THERE'S SOMETHING ABOUT A COWBOY

RICH AMOOI

DEDICATION

I LOVE MY WIFE!

CHAPTER ONE

"He's the epitome of everything I don't want in a man." Amy Weaver eyed the tall, well-built cowboy in the blue and gray plaid flannel shirt standing next to Buckshot, the mechanical bull. She downed the rest of her Blue Moon beer and shook her head. "Look at him."

"I am, I am." Jennie licked her lips and stared at the man like he was a slice of warm apple pie with a scoop of vanilla ice cream. "Yum, yum, yummy."

Amy passed her niece a cocktail napkin. "You're drooling."

It had to be their age difference, obviously, because she wasn't seeing what Jennie was seeing.

Or maybe Amy was trying her best to ignore it.

It didn't matter.

At the ripe old age of forty-five, Amy had no doubts she was the oldest person at the Double Deuce bar. She felt more out of place than a vegetarian at a weenie roast. Sure, Amy loved the country music playing through the sound system. And even at her age it was still hard to resist riding the

1

mechanical bull. It brought back memories of growing up in Julian, California. Climbing the apple trees on the family farm. Barrel racing with her high school rodeo club. Mentoring at the 4-H Club. The small town life.

And her dad she'd been avoiding.

The only reason Amy had agreed to go to that bar was because her twenty-two-year-old niece had called her an hour earlier saying she was ready to put herself out there again and needed Amy's support. It had been a couple of months since Jennie's fiancé had called off their wedding by text message. She wanted to have a drink or two with Amy during Happy Hour to celebrate coming out of her "two-month-funk" and moving on with her life. Amy hadn't been in the mood to go to a cowboy bar, but she would do anything for her niece.

"That shirt looks like it wants to bust open from the pressure around his chest," Jennie said, appearing to be completely recovered from her breakup. "And my-oh-my-oh-my, I love a man in Wranglers."

"Those aren't Wranglers," Amy said, glancing at the tight jeans surrounding the man's muscular legs. "That's denim-colored Saran Wrap. I swear I can see his marble collection."

Jennie laughed and pushed another shot of Patrón in Amy's direction. "You need to loosen up."

Amy downed the tequila and glanced toward the man again. Okay, she may have been exaggerating a little about not thinking he was attractive. She had to admit that the wavy strands peeking out from underneath his Stetson were kind of cute, but there was something about that cowboy that was odd. It was like he was too well put-together. For one, his shirt looked ironed. What normal man ironed his shirts?

Then there was the stubble on his face that seemed to be

the perfect length of sexy—if she were to think he was sexy, which she didn't. He looked like a model from a cowboy magazine, and most of those models weren't real cowboys, so he wasn't fooling anyone.

Jennie slid another shot toward Amy. "Have another. It'll make me feel better."

Amy stared at the shot. "Let me get this straight . . . I drink more and it makes *you* feel better? Exactly how does that work?"

"Simple. When you drink you loosen up. And when you're loose—"

"I don't want to be loose."

"Not *that* kind of loose, although you sure could use some, if you know what I mean."

Amy slid the shot of tequila back toward Jennie. "Use some *what*?"

Jennie tilted her head in the direction of the cowboy by the bull. "Some of *that*."

"I don't need any of that."

"Yes—you do. You're cranky and lonely. You need *a lot* of that."

Ouch.

Sure, Amy would admit she was cranky, but lonely?

She was too busy to be lonely.

As for the crankiness, it had everything to do with being in that cowboy bar. She'd promised herself to quit dating cowboys since she had such a poor track record with them. Being there at the Double Deuce gave Amy the heebie-jeebies. There was just too much temptation. Maybe she needed to sign up for Cowboys Anonymous. Was there such a thing? There should be.

Hi. My name is Amy Weaver and it has been two years since my last cowboy.

"You out of all people should know a few bad apples don't spoil the whole bunch," Jennie continued. "You need to get back on the horse. Just like me."

Wonderful.

She couldn't believe she was getting advice from someone half her age, someone barely old enough to drink alcohol.

"I thought I was here to help *you*," Amy said.

"We can help each other." Jennie slid the tequila closer.

Amy pointed to the shot glass. "That stuff only gets me into trouble."

"I need your support and it won't be the same if we're on different levels of inebriation. Keep up, would ya? Besides, that cowboy is going to be coming over here any minute and we need to be ready."

Amy glanced over at the man and then back to Jennie. "Why would he be coming over here?"

Jennie smiled. "Look at the two of us. I mean, why *wouldn't* he come over here?"

Amy had no idea what that meant, but luckily she didn't have to worry about that particular man, because he was an imposter.

A wannabe cowboy.

Most likely the bar hired him to socialize with women so they would hang around longer, flirt with him, and keep buying drinks. She would bet he was a starving actor.

What didn't make sense was why his boots were so scuffed.

He probably bought a used pair at the thrift store.

Amy gave in and slammed the shot of tequila.

How many shots was that? I need to cut myself off.

"I don't get it," Jennie said, staring at Amy like she had sprouted goat horns. "What is it exactly about that perfect specimen of a man that you don't like?"

"He's a fake," Amy said, sighing. "That body came from a gym, not from pitching bales and roping animals. Have you seen his biceps?"

"How could I not?" Jennie said. "I want to pet them." She slammed her shot, and then set the glass back on the counter, spinning it. "And you're wrong. He's an authentic cowboy. I can see that with my own two feet."

Amy reached over and covered Jennie's shot glass with her palm, stopping the spin. "You've obviously had enough to drink if you think your feet have eyes. Let's go." She glanced back over at the fake cowboy. She could have sworn he looked over at her.

"I'm not ready to go," Jennie said. "And for someone you have no interest in, you sure are doin' a whole bunch of ogling."

Amy crossed her arms. "I *am not* ogling. I'm analyzing."

"Yeah? Well tell me what you see."

"I see a man who works out twice a day. He avoids carbs. He drinks protein smoothies every two to three hours on the hour. His waist looks smaller than mine, which should be against the law."

She watched him as he talked to the mechanical bull operator, laughing and slapping the man on the back.

What are they talking about?

The fake cowboy slipped his hand into the leather glove and then mounted Buckshot in one swift motion, moving his backside around to settle into position.

She looked forward to watching him fly off and land flat on his butt.

His firm butt.

"He won't last five seconds on Buckshot," Amy said.

"I don't know," Jennie said. "He sure looks confident. Like he knows what he's doing."

"It's all an act. I could outride him."

"You think so?"

"I *know* so."

Jennie smiled and put two fingers in her mouth.

Her whistle silenced the bar.

Everyone looked in their direction.

Amy grabbed Jennie's arm and yanked her closer. "What are you doing?"

"Finding you a man. You've been single for too long and I'm worried."

"I don't need you to worry about me and I don't need a man."

"Hey, cowboy!" Jennie said, ignoring her aunt. "My auntie's got a proposition for you!" She pointed to Amy proudly.

The patrons in the bar cheered.

The man grinned and then slid back off the bull.

Oh, no.

"I can't believe you did that," Amy said, wondering how many years she would get in prison for killing her own niece. Hopefully, she'd have a sympathetic judge who understood that some family members just needed to be eliminated.

Jennie laughed. "Relax. He's just a cowboy."

Cowboy or not, Amy didn't want to take a chance.

"Do you still carry the engagement ring in your purse?"

Amy asked.

Jennie hesitated. "Yes, but since I'm officially over the douchebag I'm going to leave it at home starting tomorrow. Or maybe I'll sell it since he said I could do whatever I want with it." She laughed. "The guilt got to him, obviously."

Amy held out her hand. "Give it to me."

"That's not necessary. I told you. I'm going to stop carrying it around."

"It has nothing to do with that. Hand it over. Now."

Jennie huffed and then pulled the ring out of her purse, staring at it for a few seconds before handing it over.

Amy quickly slipped the ring on her finger.

"What are you up to?"

"Nothing," Amy said. "I'm engaged. Remember that."

"Engaged?" Jennie laughed. "You're not—"

"Shh! He's coming."

The cowboy swaggered in their direction, smooth and confident, like he owned the place.

Holy guacamole.

The man was even better looking up close.

He grinned and tipped his hat. "Evenin', ladies." He said *ladies* like he was talking to both of them, but his eyes were only on Amy. "A proposition, huh? I'm all ears."

Amy had to admit he did have nice ears.

His cologne was distracting her.

What was that?

Calvin Klein Leather and Lime?

You smell nice.

Jennie wrapped her arms around Amy. "I'm Jennie and this is my aunt Amy."

"A pleasure to meet you both. I'm Luke. Luke Jenkins."

"Nice to meet you, Luke. My aunt says she can outride you."

Luke arched an eyebrow and shot a glance over to the bull. Then he got his eyes back on Amy, sizing her up from head to toe. "Is that right? You ride?"

"You bet I do," Amy said. "And if it weren't for the fact that we were just leaving, I would prove it to you." She grabbed her purse and turned to Jennie. "Ready?"

Jennie shook her head. "I'm *ready* for another round of drinks. You're not going anywhere." She turned back to Luke. "So, here's the deal . . . if my aunt Amy outrides you, you buy us a round of drinks."

Amy wasn't going to ride the bull just so Jennie could get free drinks.

Luke rubbed his chin and nodded. "That sounds acceptable. And if I win?"

"Well . . . naturally, we'll buy *you* a drink."

Luke chuckled. "I appreciate that, I really do, but it's not much of an incentive. I get my drinks free since my buddy works here." He eyed Amy again. "You don't want to ride against me, anyway. Trust me."

"I'm *really* scared," Amy said, her voice dripping with sarcasm.

He probably thought she was some timid middle-aged woman who baked cookies all day, but he was so wrong. Okay, there were some days that she baked cookies—lots of cookies, in fact—but her point was she wasn't some delicate flower afraid of adventure.

"Okay, then. Forget about betting a round of drinks." Jennie looked at Amy and smiled. "If you win, my aunt will go on a date with you."

"What?" Amy said, wondering where the heck that came from.

"I'm flattered, but I'm not interested," Luke said, without missing a beat. He glanced at Amy. "No offense, ma'am."

No offense? There was enough offense in his response to fill the Grand Canyon. She had no interest whatsoever in going out with the man, but how dare he not see that she was a decent woman and a catch? He should be begging to go out with her! Then she would tell him, "Not on your life!"

"No offense taken," Amy lied. "You're not my type, either."

Luke chuckled. "Oh, I didn't mean you weren't my type."

Amy blinked. "Pardon me?"

"*You are* my type. But I have no interest in dating at this particular moment in my life."

How could she respond to that? It almost sounded like a compliment.

Why was Amy thinking about it so much?

And why did Jennie have that devious look on her face?

"I don't have any interest in dating, either," Amy said, not knowing what else to say.

"Good," Luke said, throwing her a wink. "Glad we got that cleared up."

She wasn't being a hundred percent honest. Amy was open to dating, actually. She'd been accused of being too picky on more than one occasion, and that was true. But she was technically stuck somewhere between being a spinster and an old maid, so why should she settle? That's why she was willing to wait for the right man. And the right man wasn't a cowboy.

So why was she so uptight about Luke?

He was a fake, plus he was at least ten years younger than Amy.

A cougar she was not.

"What about a kiss?" Jennie blurted out.

Both Amy and Luke stared at Jennie and then glanced at each other.

Luke's gaze dropped to Amy's lips for a brief moment and then shot back up to her eyes.

Why wasn't the man objecting?

And why wasn't Amy saying anything?

Someone must have hit the pause button on their brains.

"And I'm not talking about a kiss on the cheek," Jennie clarified, like this was actually going to happen. "It needs to be on the lips. Fifteen seconds. Minimum."

Amy couldn't remember the last time she'd shared a fifteen-second kiss. Sure, there was that one time she had kissed country singer Tim McGraw, but dreams didn't count.

She wasn't going to kiss a complete stranger, anyway. It didn't matter how sexy he was.

Wait a minute.

So she thought he was sexy now? What was going on with her? It wasn't that long ago when she didn't understand the fuss Jennie was making about Luke.

Amy glanced down at the empty shot glasses on the table.

It was the tequila.

She needed to cut herself off right then and there.

She also needed to put an end to this kissing nonsense.

"No deal," Amy said, firmly.

"What's the problem?" Jennie said. "A kiss is not as serious as a date. A kiss is . . . just a kiss."

"A kiss *is not* just a kiss."

"Listen." Jennie pointed to the speakers hanging from the ceiling in the bar. "This is a sign."

Amy listened closely to the song playing.

"Just a Kiss" by Lady Antebellum.

She glanced over at Luke, who was mighty quiet.

He threw his hands up and surrendered. "Don't look at me —I had nothing to do with that. But you do have to admit it is *quite* a coincidence. Anyway, I'll take the bet."

Amy placed her hands on her hips. "Dream. On."

Ugh. I feel punchy. He must think I'm a bitch, but how else am I supposed to protect my heart?

"I can't believe we're even having this conversation," Amy continued, shaking her head. "Okay, now I *do* need another drink."

"And I would be happy to buy you one after you outride me," Luke said, gesturing back to Buckshot.

Reverse psychology. Well played.

Essentially, Luke was daring her now.

Amy *so* wanted to prove him wrong.

She was confident she could outride him.

Luke turned to Jennie. "I'm guessing your auntie here is afraid of enjoying the kiss too much."

Amy laughed. "You're the one who would be enjoying it too much."

He arched an eyebrow. "Yeah?"

"Yeah. One of my kisses would make you forget your own name."

He stepped closer. "I can appreciate that, but Jennie would have to scrape *you* off the floor after our lips touch because I've been known to buckle knees with my . . . slow . . . deep . . . wet . . . kisses."

Amy blinked.

When was the last time she'd had a slow, deep, wet kiss?

Never—that's when.

Luke grinned when he caught Amy glancing at his lips.

Heat flooded her cheeks.

She swallowed hard.

Do not look at his full, luscious lips again.

This nonsense had to stop before she got herself in trouble.

The ring, you idiot!

Amy had completely forgotten she had stuck the engagement ring on her finger.

She held up her hand. "I'm engaged, okay? So kissing is completely inappropriate and may even be illegal in several states."

"It's my ring, actually." Jennie turned to Luke. "She's wearing it so men don't hit on her. So, as long as you don't try to pick up my auntie, you're good to go."

Amy was well aware her mouth was hanging open.

Too bad words weren't coming out.

Luke cocked an eyebrow. "You're a mighty fascinating woman, Amy. Look—this has been a hoot, but obviously you have no intention of riding the bull, engaged or not engaged, and I truly do respect your wise decision. You ladies enjoy the rest of your evening." He tipped his hat and turned back toward Buckshot.

Amy hated that smug, satisfied look on his face.

It was like he'd beaten her without having to lift a finger.

Not on her watch.

"Hold it right there, mister," Amy said. "Not so fast."

Luke stopped and swung back around, amusement in his eyes. "Yes?"

"I'll take that bet," Amy said. "Prepare to lose."

CHAPTER TWO

Amy should've already been out the door and on her way home. Instead, she was going to ride the bull against Luke. And they were betting a kiss!

Damn tequila.

There was only one thing she could do now.

She had to win.

No ifs, ands, or firm butts about it.

Don't get her wrong—Amy was confident she could beat Luke. She'd done this before many times, although usually she bet cash, not kisses. While she had attended culinary school, she'd ridden mechanical bulls against cocky cowboys to help pay the bills.

The problem was she hadn't gotten on a mechanical bull in such a long time.

Relax. You've got this. Just like riding a bike . . .

Okay, it was nothing like riding a bike, but a little positive thinking couldn't hurt.

At least she was wearing her favorite jeans.

Luke slapped the bull operator on the back. "Ed—meet Amy and Jennie."

"Pleased to meet you both," Ed said, gesturing to the bull. "You wanna take Buckshot for a spin?"

"Not me," Jennie answered. "But my auntie Amy bet Luke she could outride him."

"Really?" Ed said, glancing at Amy from head to toe.

Why did they all do that? Luke had done the same thing earlier. Like they were going to figure out Amy's physical ability or skill level by glancing at her body.

Yeah, she was petite, but they both had a big surprise coming.

Luke pointed to Buckshot. "Ladies first."

"No, no," Amy said, shaking her head. "After you. I insist."

"As you wish." Luke winked at her and then mounted Buckshot. After settling into position, he grabbed ahold of the rope with one hand and lifted his off-hand in the air.

"Ready," Luke said.

The guy didn't waste any time at all.

"Here we go," Ed said, pressing the start button.

The bull started to move slowly. Even recreational riders and drunk people typically didn't have a problem with the first or second level. Luke didn't appear to be fazed at all as Ed advanced the level again. Even when he cranked up the buck-and-spin speed and changed up the spin direction, Luke still appeared confident and in control. Relaxed, even.

Still, Amy was convinced Luke was an imposter. Skill wasn't keeping him on that bull. It had to be those powerful legs of his. That would only get him so far. A couple more levels and Luke would be off the bull and flat on his back.

Any second now . . .

"Quit teasing me with the kiddie ride," Luke yelled out.

Or not.

Amy had to admit this was a little disconcerting.

Luke was heading to a level she had only done once before and that was years ago.

Not good.

She didn't want to lose, and she especially didn't want to kiss the man. Sure, there were probably far worse things in life, but she couldn't think of any at the moment.

Ed cranked it up more.

Jennie cheered. "Go, Luke! Yahooooo!"

Amy glared at her niece. "What are you doing?"

"Encouraging him—of course. There's nothing I want more than to see you two kissing."

"I don't get it. You were the one practically undressing him with your eyeballs earlier. Why aren't you interested in him?"

"In him? No way. Sure, he's some serious eye candy, no doubt, but you know I prefer the nerdy type. Give me a computer engineer and I'll be naked before you can say hard disk."

Amy shook her head and turned her attention back to Luke as he lost control on level six.

Ed hit the quick-stop button to slow the bull as Luke flew off the side, landing on his back.

He quickly jumped to his feet and brushed off his jeans.

Jennie moved to the rail's edge and high-fived Luke. "You rocked it."

"Thanks," Luke said, turning and locking eyes with Amy. "I guess you're up unless you've changed your mind. It's nothing to be embarrassed about."

"You might want to get that credit card ready," Amy said,

stepping past Luke and grabbing a pair of small leather gloves from Ed.

A few seconds later, she was up on the bull. She pointed her boots slightly out and squeezed her legs around the bull. She made sure her weight was centered, lifted her off-hand in the air, and took in a deep breath, letting it out slowly. "Ready."

Ed pressed the start button. "Okay, good luck."

The bull started to move slowly, dipping forward and then backward, as it did with Luke. A little bit of bucking and spinning and they were off to the races.

Amy had to admit she had missed being on top of a mechanical bull, but this wasn't the time to get sentimental. She needed to focus on her balance, because balance was everything. Buckshot was really testing her already, bucking and spinning, and switching directions faster and faster.

And she was only at level five.

One more level and she would be even with Luke, then she would just need at a few seconds at that level to beat him.

Hang on. You've got this.

Ed cranked it up to the next level and Amy felt the difference immediately.

It had been a long time since she had ridden at this intensity. Too long.

Now she was holding on for dear life.

Two or three more seconds at this level to win.

"Yes!" Amy yelled out, confident she beat Luke's time. And it couldn't have come any sooner because she was thrown from Buckshot spectacularly, doing a flip, and almost landing on her head. She lay there in the foam pit on her back for a moment, staring up at the ceiling, laughing.

She did it. She beat Luke.

There was nothing like the feeling of beating a cocky cowboy.

The entire bar erupted in cheers and whistles for Amy.

It was an exhilarating moment, especially seeing the defeated look on her niece's face.

"Luke wins!" Ed called out.

Jennie sprang to life. "Yes!"

The entire bar started booing.

Amy jumped to her feet. "What? No way. That's not possible!"

"See for yourself," Ed said, pointing to the electric monitor.

Amy took a few steps toward Ed, glancing down at Luke's time, then her time.

"How could that be?"

She was sure she had won.

"That was so close," Ed said. "He beat you by one second. It was a mighty good ride, Amy."

Mighty good wasn't good enough.

Maybe the average forty-five-year-old woman couldn't have done what she had done, but that didn't make Amy feel any better. She should've done better. Instead, she'd lost the bet.

She waited for Luke to gloat.

To declare himself a winner.

To pucker up.

But when she finally glanced in his direction, the expression on Luke's face wasn't one of satisfaction at all. It was one of sympathy.

"You were amazing, Auntie Amy," Jennie said, giving her a hug.

She glanced up again at Luke, who was still quiet.

Why wasn't he asking to collect his prize of the kiss?

A deal was a deal, and he had won fair and square.

She had no idea what was going through his mind, but she would kiss him and then high-tail it out of there.

Amy forced a smile and held out her hand. "Congratulations. You win a kiss."

"Thanks," Luke said, shaking Amy's hand. "I sure am looking forward to forgetting my name."

CHAPTER THREE

It was funny how fast the evening had gone from lame to looking up.

Luke had come to the Double Deuce to meet a couple of investors who had been thinking about buying the building next door and turning it into the premier barbecue restaurant in San Diego. He'd been contacted because he was an award-winning barbecue pitmaster. One of the best in the business, he'd appeared on national television and had more awards than you could shake a skewer at. After the investors learned that Luke insisted on a very expensive open-air kitchen, their interest in the project cooled and they said they'd get back to him. He was pretty sure they'd changed their minds and didn't want to spend the money. Luke had been ready to let off some steam on Buckshot when a woman from across the bar had yelled in his direction.

But she wasn't the one who had caught his eye.

It was the woman next to her.

Intriguing, fascinating, beautiful Amy.

Luke wanted to know more about her. Sure, she was one of the prettiest ladies he'd ever laid eyes on, but right now his stimulation wasn't physical. Her tenacity was impressive. And she was feisty as hell. Maybe it was the whole package. Who knew?

Now she was going to kiss him.

Just like that.

Too bad she didn't seem happy about it.

Amy looked like she was being forced to walk the plank, but he could see a sparkle of slight interest in those beautiful hazel eyes of hers. She was fighting certain urges.

"Before we do this, let's establish some ground rules," Amy said.

Luke stifled a laugh. "Rules in kissing are about as normal as a two-headed pig."

"Number one . . ." Amy ignored his comment. "No touching. Number two—"

Luke held up his hand. "Hold up a minute there. Can we go back to number one?"

Amy blew out a breath. "I knew this wasn't going to be easy. What's not clear about no touching?"

"Well . . . I'm not a rocket scientist or an anatomy teacher, but I'm pretty sure it's impossible to kiss without our lips touching."

Amy sighed. "Of course the lips have to touch. I'm talking about the rest of our bodies. No touching, *AKA* keep your hands to yourself. And all other body parts for that matter. Can I move on?"

"Yes, ma'am, but keep in mind the bar closes in three hours."

"Not funny. Number two, this is only going to be a

fifteen-second kiss. Jennie will keep track of the time." She paused, most likely thinking Luke was going to say something, but he kept his mouth shut. "And number three, no tongue."

No tongue?

What the hell kind of rule was that?

Who ever heard of a kiss without tongue?

He specialized in tongue!

Luke wanted to protest but bit his tongue, since it wasn't going to be much use to him.

Amy crossed her arms. "You're not saying anything. Please nod your head or wave a hand in the air if you understand my rules. They are not negotiable."

Luke chuckled and glanced over at Jennie. "Is she always this hostile?"

Jennie nodded. "Must be the lack of kissing with tongue."

Amy stepped closer to Luke. "Are you ready or not?"

She glanced up at Luke.

Beautiful.

He grinned and leaned down closer to her. "Ready."

"I'm taking the lead. *I'm* kissing *you.*"

"So many rules . . ." He eyed her lips.

Why was this kissing foreplay a total turn on?

It had to be the anticipation.

Amy reached up and lost her balance, accidentally brushing her lips against his.

That was sexy as hell.

Do that again, please.

She stepped back for a second to regain her composure. "That didn't happen."

"Nope. It did not. But I would have no problem at all if it happened again."

Amy stepped forward again and reached up, finally pressing her lips to his. It was sweet and gentle. Her lips were soft.

So soft.

Their mouths fit together perfectly. It was such a simple kiss, but Luke loved it. How could a kiss without tongue be so good?

Luke couldn't help but wonder what it would be like with tongue because kissing her was a full body experience. This made no sense at all since his hands were behind his back and their bodies and tongues weren't even touching.

Only lips!

Luke's heart rate kicked up a notch when he gently nibbled on Amy's bottom lip. It wasn't planned, it just happened, so hopefully he wasn't going to get kicked in the nuts. Technically, he didn't break any rules. She said no tongue, but she didn't say no teeth.

What came next was most surprising.

Amy moaned and opened her mouth slightly.

An invitation?

He wasn't sure, so he proceeded with caution.

Luke opened his mouth a tad to see how she would respond.

That's when Amy wrapped her arms around his neck and kissed him harder.

With tongue.

They were kissing with tongues.

And *she* was the one who'd initiated it, so there was no chance of Amy castrating him today.

An explosion of desire ripped through Luke's body.

He grabbed Amy by the waist and pulled her against him, then deepened the kiss.

She said she wanted to take the lead, but now he was the one in the driver's seat and this was the Indy 500. No. This was heaven.

Their tongues were dancing to the beat of the Garth Brooks song blasting from the speakers. The kiss was only supposed to last fifteen seconds, but they surely had to be closing in on a minute. Was Jennie still there? That didn't matter, either. Luke sure as heck wasn't going to be the one who broke off the kiss. He was going to close down the bar with this kiss.

If only . . .

Amy pulled away and touched her lips with her fingers, a dazed look on her face. Not a surprise, since he was just as blown away as she was.

"Hot damn," Luke mumbled.

"Hot damn, indeed," Jennie said, her gaze bouncing back and forth between Luke and Amy. "All hell broke loose with your mouths, and that was so totally hot."

Jennie's assessment of the kiss was spot on.

Totally hot.

And he had no doubts that Amy felt the same way.

Or not . . .

Amy grabbed her purse. "I said no touching. I said no tongue."

"Your tongue started it."

"Let's go, Jennie."

Luke stared at her.

The woman was crazy.

He wasn't imagining things. She had started it. And she'd kissed him back.

"Jennie?" Amy said when she noticed her niece wasn't moving. "We're leaving."

Jennie sighed. "Fine."

Amy turned and walked toward the door, not saying another word to either of them.

Jennie crinkled her nose. "Sorry about that. It was nice to meet you."

"The pleasure was mine," Luke said, watching as Jennie followed Amy out.

Ed approached Luke and slapped him on the back. "What the heck was that all about?"

"I have no idea," Luke said. "Is it possible to be confused and turned on at the same time?"

Ed nodded. "A woman will do that to ya."

Luke nodded. "Yeah . . ."

"Forget about her."

Right.

Like it would be that easy.

That was a kiss for the ages.

Luke wasn't sure if it would ever be possible to forget Amy.

Amy tossed her keys on the kitchen counter and sighed, glad to be back home after grabbing a taxi from the bar. She kicked off her shoes, slid onto the sofa and grabbed the remote, turning on the television. Maybe a few reruns of *The Golden Girls* on the Hallmark Channel would take her mind off things. She was in luck because it was one of her favorite

THERE'S SOMETHING ABOUT A COWBOY

episodes, the one where Dorothy, Blanche, and Rose stopped by a bar and are mistakenly arrested for being prostitutes.

Okay, maybe it would be harder than she thought to get distracted because her mind was back on the bar, the bull, and that kiss with Luke. She still couldn't believe what had happened.

"What was I thinking?" Amy asked herself as she touched her lips again.

And how had she gotten roped into a bull-riding contest?

"I should have known better."

Luke was bad news from the moment she'd laid eyes on him but she'd still taken the bet, and then lost. Then she lost control of her libido when a simple peck turned into a teenage make-out session.

She was forty-five years old!

And what was he? Twenty-eight? Thirty, maybe?

He was practically a baby!

But she'd been an even bigger baby when she'd walked out of the bar without even looking back.

She shook her head in embarrassment when she replayed the entire scene in her head.

Her behavior was uncalled for. Luke had done nothing wrong.

Amy had gotten scared.

Scared of the way he'd been looking at her.

Scared of the way she'd been feeling when she kissed him.

Because that kiss was . . .

Wow.

Was there a way of describing what had happened between her and Luke?

Magical?

No.

This wasn't a Disney movie.

It was *Bull Durham*, *The Graduate*, and *Kung Fu Panda* rolled into one.

It was like her brain had short-circuited the moment their lips connected.

That's why she had broken her own rule.

She had said no tongue, but she wanted it.

And he got the hint and gave it to her.

That's when the rest of the rules flew out the window.

Thankfully, the buzzing of Amy's cell phone pulled her thoughts away from Luke and the kiss.

"Hi, Grandpa Leo," she answered, a smile forming on her face.

He always made her smile, no matter what was going on in her life.

"How's my little sweetie pie?"

Grandpa Leo was the only one in the world who could get away with calling her that. He'd been doing it ever since she was a baby.

"Good timing because I just walked in the door and turned on *The Golden Girls*," Amy said.

"Have I ever told you I have a thing for Bea Arthur?"

"You'd better be careful or Grams is going to—"

"I heard that!" Grandma Betty said, picking up the other phone line in their house. "Don't make me come over there, Leo Weaver."

"I dare you. You probably don't even know where I am."

"Where else? On your recliner with the remote in your hand."

"Very impressive. Since your granny GPS is working so

well, why don't you bring me a piece of that delicious apple pie with some of that slow-Chernobyl vanilla ice cream."

"It's slow-churned, nincompoop."

Amy laughed. "You two knock it off."

Grandpa Leo and Grandma Betty were always bickering back and forth. The average person listening might think they were arguing, but it was all an act. Amy didn't know two people who were more in love than them.

"We can't wait to see you this weekend," Grandpa Leo said.

"I can't wait to see you, too."

Every year Amy headed back home to Julian, California in September for the Julian Country Fair and her grandpa's birthday. This year was special because he was turning ninety.

"Make sure you bring your fiancé," Grandpa Leo said.

Amy stared at the phone.

What was her grandpa talking about?

Was he finally starting to lose his faculties?

"Sweetie pie?" Grandpa Leo said. "Are you there?"

"I'm here," Amy replied. "I'm trying to figure out why you would think I have a fiancé."

"Grandma and I saw you on Facebook kissing the cowboy. We also saw the ring on your finger. Mighty impressive."

"He's so handsome," Grandma Betty said. "You certainly were getting all touchy-feely with him in public, which I guess is not much of a surprise considering what a strapping young man he is."

"He must love you somethin' awful to get you a rock that big," Grandpa Leo said. "Unless . . . are you pregnant?"

"What?" Amy said, glancing down at the ring that was still

stuck on her finger. "No! I'm not pregnant and *I don't* have a fiancé. What picture are you talking about?"

"The one Jennie posted from the Double Deuce," Grandpa Leo said. "Right in front of Buckshot."

That's why her niece had been so quiet during the kiss. She'd been taking pictures!

Just when Amy thought things couldn't get any more embarrassing, there was a picture of her kissing Luke on Facebook for the whole world to see. Okay, she didn't have that many friends on Facebook, but Jennie did. People could share the photo and make it go viral.

This wasn't happening.

"Hold on a minute," Amy said, sending a text to Jennie demanding she remove the photo from Facebook. A few seconds later, the reply came back from her niece.

Jennie: What? I thought I posted the picture of you on the bull. So sorry! Removing it now.

At least Jennie wasn't passed out drunk and was able to do damage control.

Jennie: I deleted it. So sorry, Auntie Amy. By the way, my taxi driver was so cute. Was yours?

"Okay, I'm back," Amy said, ignoring her niece's text for now. "Where were we?"

"We were talking about your cowboy lover," Grams said.

"That's all I ever wanted was for you to be happy with *a real man* before I kicked the bucket," Grandpa Leo said.

"Sorry to break the news to you both, but he's not my fiancé."

"Now, don't you go joking around like that," Grandpa Leo said. "You never know when I'm going to keel over from this old heart of mine. My A-orca is not what it used to be."

"Aorta."

"That, too. Sad things make my heart hurt. I feel something funny going on right now."

"Here we go again," Grams said. "Knock it off, Leo. There's nothing wrong with your heart."

Grandpa Leo was known as "The Great Exaggerator" in the family. Yes, he did have a slight heart condition, but he used it so much as an excuse that no one ever knew if he was lying or dying.

"I can't wait to meet him!" Grandpa Leo added, suddenly feeling more upbeat. "I insist that you bring the cowboy to the party and I won't take no for an answer. What's his name?"

Amy didn't want to upset his fragile heart but taking Luke to the party was not going to happen.

"His name is Luke. And I told you, Grandpa, he's not my—"

"Nathan is going to be at the party," Grandpa Leo blurted out. "In case my poor heart wasn't a good enough reason to bring Luke."

"What?" Amy said, feeling her pulse bang in her head at the mention of her ex. "Who invited Nathan?"

"Your father, of course."

Yet another person Amy needed to add to her list of people to kill.

"Nauseating Nathan is more like it," Grandpa Leo added. "Sure you won't let me get rid of him? I'll take him out to the other side of the pasture and—"

"Grandpa," Amy said.

He was only half-joking, but it was the other half that scared her.

"Fine, fine," Grandpa Leo said. "He's a master at sucking up to your father. Hear that slurping? That's him again. The man could suck a Big Mac through a screen door."

Amy's father, Greg, believed that she should be with a cowboy. He also believed that the cowboy should be Nathan, even though they had broken up two years ago. The sad part was, Amy was sure Nathan still believed they belonged together, too. Whatever happened to moving on? He still sent her flowers on her birthday. And every year when Amy returned home for the country fair and Grandpa Leo's birthday, Nathan happened to be at the ranch.

Not that Nathan was a horrible person, but they wanted different things. He wanted Amy to be a housewife, and she wanted him to go far, far away.

Suddenly, she wasn't so excited to go back to Julian. She had hoped this would be the year when Nathan would finally love a woman who wasn't Amy.

"Nathan will go away with Luke on your arm," Grandpa Leo said. "Fiancé or not, Luke needs to be there."

"Why do you say that?" Amy said.

"Simple. Once Nathan meets Luke and sees that the two of you are engaged, you'll take the wind right out of his sails. You've never brought any of the other cowboys home for the festival, and that's always given Nathan hope that he could win you back. With Luke there, it won't happen. Nathan will be gone. He may sniff around and make sure Luke is the real deal, may even challenge him to a duel or something, but then he'll be gone with the wind."

Amy sat up on the sofa, muted *The Golden Girls*, and pondered the situation. Is that all it would take to finally get Nathan out of her life for good? And would her dad finally see that she was able to choose a man for herself? It was like her dad was obsessed with her being with Nathan. Could she show up with Luke and shut them both up for good? It seemed too easy.

She glanced down again at the engagement ring stuck on her finger and tried to twist it off. Was it stuck on her finger for a reason? What if she left it on? It was tempting, that was for sure, but even if she did think it was a good idea there was one big problem. Luke would never go for it.

Unless . . .

Maybe Amy could pay him.

Starving actors always needed money.

He could pose as her fake cowboy fiancé.

Then Nathan would go away.

Then maybe her dad would lighten up and get off her case about being with Nathan.

Grandpa Leo could blame his fragile heart on something else.

None of them would ever know Luke was an imposter because he played the part of a cowboy well. From riding the bull to that sexy kiss.

Stop it.

Amy needed to get that kiss out of her head because it was

wrong to think she would get another one. She didn't want another one, no matter how good it was.

"Are you there?" Grandpa Leo said.

"Yes," Amy said. "I'm . . . thinking."

"No need to do that when I can do the thinking for you. The bottom line is, if you don't bring Luke to my birthday this weekend, you can bring him to my memorial."

"Grandpa! Don't say that."

The Great Exaggerator was in top form this evening.

Amy wondered about her options. Sure, Grandpa was always exaggerating, but what if she was the one who sent him to his grave? She would never recover from that, she was sure of it. But even if her Grandpa Leo was bluffing, she could finally put Nathan behind her and close that chapter of her life, once and for all.

Amy slid off the couch and paced back and forth in the kitchen. She always got nervous when she was going to do something that could backfire in her face.

That's right—she wanted to do it.

"You've got nothing to lose except your dignity," she mumbled to herself.

"What's that?" Grandpa Leo said.

Oh, wait. She'd lost her dignity when she'd decided to ride the bull against Luke.

Maybe she didn't have anything to lose.

"You know I don't agree with your grandpa much, sweetie, but this time he may be right," Grams said.

"This time?" Grandpa Leo said. "I'm always right. She needs to bring Luke. That's all I want for my birthday. Promise me you'll bring him."

The idea sounded crazy.

It also sounded like it might work.

What other options did she have?

She didn't have any.

"Okay," Amy said. "I'll do it."

"That's wonderful!" Grams said.

"That's my girl," Grandpa Leo said. "I'm feeling better already!"

After Amy disconnected the call, she leaned against the kitchen counter, wondering what she had gotten herself into. She couldn't blame it on the tequila this time since the buzz was wearing off.

"I've lost my mind," she said to the empty room, sighing.

It didn't matter.

She'd already made the decision and there was no turning back now that she had promised Grandpa Leo.

Tomorrow, Amy would go back to the Double Deuce and offer Mr. Luke Jenkins money to be her fake fiancé for the week. Then Nathan would finally be out of her life.

Hopefully, it would be that easy.

CHAPTER FOUR

The next night, Amy pulled five different outfits from the closet and threw them on the bed. She held each one up against her body in front of the mirror.

Nope. Nope. Nope. Nope. And . . . nope.

None of them looked good. She frowned and hung them back up in the closet, then pulled out another five, also laying them on the bed.

Why is this so difficult?

Amy was trying to figure out what to wear to the Double Deuce to make Luke the offer but was having the hardest time. Why did she feel nervous, like she was going on a date?

It's not a date.

Not even close to a date.

It was a business meeting.

In a bar, albeit.

Maybe that was the problem. She needed something that wasn't too conservative since she was going to a fun, casual place, but not too sexy to give Luke the wrong idea.

She had to be clear that this was business. Amy would make the offer. Luke would be her fake fiancé. Then they would go their separate ways.

Nothing more. Nothing less. End of story.

There was no reason Luke would say no, unless his schedule wouldn't allow it.

In the end, she decided on the jeans she had worn the night before, along with a white silk blouse and her favorite boots.

Tonight would be different.

No drinking.

No bull riding.

No kissing.

Thirty minutes later she pulled her maroon Ford Fusion into the Double Deuce parking lot and turned off the engine, staring through the windshield at the front door.

"Here goes nothing," she said to herself, taking a deep breath before getting out of the car.

Once inside the Double Deuce, she glanced around the place for Luke. He'd be easy to spot, considering his size. A few seconds later, she spotted a well-built man with his back to her, talking to a group of four women by the bar. Already flirting with the ladies to get them to buy more drinks. It had to be him. Same build. Same hat.

She walked in his direction, but then stopped when she glanced down at his other assets.

Not the same butt.

Okay, she felt a little shallow that she remembered his butt, but she had seen at least three other women checking it out the night before, so she wasn't alone.

Speaking of alone, Amy was happy that Jennie wasn't there this time to get her into trouble.

She scanned the entire place and didn't see Luke anywhere. Maybe he didn't start work yet or was in the bathroom. Was it his night off? She hadn't thought of that. Ed, the mechanical bull operator, would know for sure.

Amy walked over toward the bull riding pit as a woman flew off Buckshot.

"You're back!" Ed called out, a surprised look on his face. "What a surprise, considering the way you took off out of here."

"Sorry about that." Amy shrugged. "I wasn't having the best night." She gestured around the bar. "Is Luke working?"

Ed hesitated. "Luke doesn't work here."

That was the last thing she expected him to say.

How could he not work there anymore?

Oh, no.

Luke must have gotten fired for kissing Amy.

He was there to make it fun for the ladies so they drank more, but it made sense that the bar had a hands-off policy. He'd broken the rule because of her. She didn't know the man, but she felt horrible.

Ed pointed to Amy's head. "I can see the wheels spinning there in that pretty little head of yours. Why would you think Luke worked here?"

"He wasn't working last night?"

"Nope."

Unbelievable. She never confirmed he worked there. She'd assumed.

Amy had to do something. "Do you know where I can find him? You're friends with him, right?"

Ed nodded. "Sure am. He's at the Hillcrest Theater."

Of course. Amy wondered what type of show he was performing in. Shakespeare? Contemporary? Melodrama? A musical. He was on the cocky side, so she wouldn't be surprised if it was a comedy.

Amy thanked Ed, turned down his invitation to ride Buckshot again, and drove to the Hillcrest Theater. Her timing was perfect. She pulled into a spot across the street from the theater as Luke swaggered out the front door. The cowboy outfit from last night was replaced with a navy blazer, white shirt, and a red tie. Tonight, she could see his full head of wavy black hair.

Beautiful hair. Versatile with his wardrobe. Dapper.

If she were being honest, she would say the man was even more attractive tonight than he'd been last night, but she would scratch that thought from her brain.

Amy got out of her car and approached Luke as he opened the door to his Ford F150 pickup truck. "Hey."

Luke swung around and froze, then a smile formed on his face. "Hey. Didn't think I'd ever see you again."

She shrugged. "I guess I'm a glutton for punishment."

Luke chuckled and closed the door, leaning against the truck. "Are you here to proposition me again?"

"I am."

He nodded and his smile grew wider. "I was hoping you would say that."

Amy stared at that sexy grin of his for a long beat, wondering if this would be one of those monumental mistakes she would remember for the rest of her life.

Luke had come out of a meeting with a local restauranteur who wanted to turn the Hillcrest Theater into a Murder Mystery Dinner Theater with an extensive barbecue menu. Everything sounded great until the man told Luke he wouldn't have complete creative control over the menu.

That was a deal breaker.

Luke wished he would have known that ahead of time because he hated wearing ties.

Not having creative control over the menu was the reason Luke was currently out of a job. He'd had a great job as executive chef at an upscale barbecue joint, but then the owners sold the restaurant to someone who wanted to completely change the menu. The exact menu he'd spent months perfecting and the one that had brought in huge crowds almost every night. It didn't make sense why they had wanted to mess with a good thing, so he didn't agree to it and was out of a job.

Luke's energy was low, but he needed to keep a positive mind and know a great job was headed his way. Luckily, the sight of lovely Amy got his blood pumping again, like a double shot of espresso. It had only been twenty-four hours since he'd seen her at the Double Deuce, but she seemed a lot prettier. Less hostile too, which was a good thing.

"How was the show?" Amy finally spoke.

Luke stared at her for a moment and then glanced back at the theater.

She was kidding.

"A real tear-jerker," Luke said, willing to play along. "Two thumbs up."

Amy nodded. "Good."

She was acting weird.

What she was doing there and how she had found him was

still a mystery to Luke, but it didn't matter. She'd been on his mind nonstop since the kiss last night and he certainly wasn't going to complain, although she was very quiet at the moment.

"So . . . the proposition?" Luke said, curious about what was on the pretty lady's mind.

"Yeah, that," Amy said. "I guess I should come out with it."

"Not a bad idea," Luke said, eying her hand. "You still have the ring on."

Amy glanced down at her hand and spun the one-carat solitaire, round-cut diamond ring around her finger a couple of times. "It's still stuck. That's kind of why I'm here. Let me see how I can put this." She glanced down the street and then back to Luke. "I want to offer you a job."

Luke liked the sound of that. He wasn't a slacker and was always ready for more work. Anything to keep from dipping into his savings.

He was ready to work for Amy, whatever the job entailed.

"I'm available to start tomorrow morning," Luke said. "Eight sharp, if that works for you."

Amy arched an eyebrow. "I haven't even told you about the job."

"It doesn't matter."

"It doesn't?"

She looked quite surprised by that, but he had bills to pay like anyone else.

"I can do anything and everything inside and outside of a house," Luke said. "Repairs. Remodeling. I can also cook up meat on the barbecue like nobody's business. I can be your personal chef. Whatever you want."

"Anything?" she asked.

"Anything."

"Okay . . ." She hesitated. "I . . . uh . . . well . . . I have this situation."

"What kind of situation?" Luke asked.

"Well . . . I . . . uh . . . . I should just say it."

"Not a bad idea . . ."

"Okay then." She watched the city bus go by. "I want you to pretend to be my fiancé for the week."

Now it was his turn to stare.

Her fiancé?

Maybe he misheard her because of the noise from the bus.

What rhymed with fiancé?

Disarray. Saturday. Beyoncé.

"Well?" Amy said.

"Sorry," he said, realizing he couldn't even think of one single Beyoncé song. "It sounded like you said you wanted me to be your fiancé for the week."

"That's what I said."

She'd obviously hit her head hard when she fell off Buckshot last night.

"Then I have three words for you," Luke said. "No. Can. Do."

"You said you'd do whatever I wanted."

"Not that."

Amy looked offended. "Why not? You don't even know the details. It will be the easiest money you've ever made."

He shook his head. "I don't like to deceive people. Call me crazy, but I think it's wrong."

"It's for a good cause."

Luke crossed his arms. "Fine. Give me the details."

"Okay . . . My parents live in Julian, so we would be going there."

"Apples . . ."

She nodded. "We have a family business called Pie in the Sky. We've got an apple farm and we sell fresh apple pies. Anyway, we'll go to the Julian Country Fair, my grandpa's ninetieth birthday party, and—"

"Why do you need a fiancé?"

"It's complicated."

"Un-complicate it for me."

She sighed. "There are several reasons, but the main one is my ex is going to be there and he's still in love with me. Or he's not in love with me, but he's obsessed with me. Or maybe it's my dad who wants him to be with me."

"And you don't love him anymore?"

She shook her head. "Not in a long time."

"Why don't you tell him you don't love him?"

"I have. He doesn't believe me. Especially since my dad keeps telling him I haven't met anyone new since our breakup. Anyway, none of that matters, as far as you're concerned. This is a business opportunity for you. What do you say? Like I said, it'll be easy *and* I will pay you."

"How much?"

She thought about it for a few seconds. "Five hundred dollars."

Luke laughed. "For a whole week? Not enough."

"Last night all you got was a kiss, and you were fine with that, but five hundred bucks is not enough?"

He grinned. "That was different." He glanced down at her lips again. "Now, if you want to negotiate only in kisses, that's another story. Let's start at a thousand kisses and go from there."

"Dream on." Amy pointed to his eyes and shook her finger. "And don't do that."

"What?"

"Don't look at me that way," Amy said.

"Well, then don't be so pretty."

She looked serious.

Even a little desperate.

He was always a sucker for a damsel in distress.

A pang of sympathy punched Luke right in the gut, but he was curious about something.

"Why did you leave the bar like that?" Luke said. "You ran out like the place was on fire."

"I know, I know. I'm sorry."

"What were you afraid of?"

Amy perked up. "I'll tell you after you're my fake fiancé for the week."

He studied her. "I don't know. I need some groveling while I think about it."

She placed her hands on her hips.

She looked so cute when she didn't get her way.

"Fine," Amy said. "You . . . are an *amazing* man. I misjudged you. You're *so* intelligent."

"I like this. Please continue."

"Have I told you how manly you are? Manly, manly, manly."

"Triple points for that one, but I need a little more."

Amy sighed. "You're soooo good-looking, even for someone I want to kill."

He stifled a laugh. "Love it—except the last part. More."

"Your ego needs a lot of stroking."

"Why, yes. Yes, it does."

"And your truck is so big," she continued, looking like she was growing tired of this game. "I'm sure it's compensating for your small—"

"Stop right there," Luke said, holding up his hand and chuckling at the feisty woman. "I'll take the job."

Amy jerked her head back. "You will?"

"Yup," Luke said. "Two thousand dollars."

Amy stood up straight, looking like she was about to blow a fuse. "Two thousand dollars is insane. Five hundred is more than fair."

"I'll have to disagree. We're talkin' twenty-four hours a day for seven days. That's like three bucks an hour. *Below* minimum wage. You want me to report you to the US Department of Labor? You can do better than that."

"You want to get paid while you're sleeping?" Amy asked.

"Yes. Two grand. Take it or leave it."

Amy paced back and forth and then turned to Luke. "Seven-fifty."

"Fifteen hundred."

"One *thousand* dollars," Amy huffed.

"Twelve hundred bucks," Luke said. "Final offer."

Amy stared at him again.

She sure stared a lot.

"Done," she said, holding out her hand. "Half up front, half when you complete the task."

Luke stared at her hand for a moment and then accepted it, holding on tight. "You can pay me in full at the end."

Amy hesitated. "Okay . . . Thank you. I appreciate your help. Now that that is settled, I have some rules."

"Why am I not surprised?"

"Rule number one, let go of my hand."

Luke glanced down at her hand. "Oh . . ." He grinned. "I must have forgotten about that."

"Of course, you did. Rule number two, turn off the charm."

He thought about it. "So, you're saying you find me charming?"

"I didn't say that. You did."

"You did, too."

"Number three, no kissing and no touching, which also means no sex."

Luke smirked. "I get it—you're a virgin. I can respect your—"

"And no joking."

"Is there anything I'm allowed to do?"

Amy nodded. "Yes. Remember the rules *and* be the best fake fiancé you can be. You need to be convincing while you're on the farm. My dad thinks that anyone who can't rope and ride is a pantywaist, so I just need to be sure. How comfortable are you as a cowboy?"

That had to be the strangest question ever coming from a woman's mouth. Of course, he was comfortable in his own skin. Comfortable as hell. How else was he going to feel? She must have been judging him by the jacket and tie he was wearing, which would be wrong, because he always preferred his jeans and boots. Hell yeah, he was comfortable as a cowboy.

Luke grew up on his grandparents' ranch and was riding ponies at the age of three, graduating up to real horses at the age of four. He had done every ranch job imaginable for his weekly allowance. At a young age he had already learned how to feed cattle, pitch manure, collect eggs from the hens, fixing, hauling, mowing, you name it. In his late teens he had worked as a ranch hand while he perfected his barbecue recipes at night. He truly believed all those things shaped him into who he was today. He couldn't be any more comfortable as a cowboy.

"You don't have to worry about me," Luke answered, confident he could handle whatever she threw at him.

"Good," Amy said. "Make sure you pack jeans and boots to wear every day. And the Stetson. Can't forget that."

"I would never . . ." He chuckled, wondering why the woman was telling him how to dress.

"I think we're on the same page then."

"While we're at it, I've got a few rules of my own," Luke said.

Amy glared at him. "I hired you, so you can forget about—"

"Number one, you can throw all your rules out the window."

"What?"

"Well, except for the sex rule. I'm good with that one and I think that's a good call. But if you want me to be convincing we'll need to touch, we'll need to kiss, *and* I'll need to be charming. It's not like I can turn that off, anyway. It's one hundred percent natural." He winked.

"No deal."

"Then you have yourself a good evening," Luke said, turning to open to door to his truck.

"Wait!"

Luke swung back around. "Yes, ma'am. How can I help you?"

"I thought we already had a deal? You can't back out now. I need you. It has to be you because my niece posted pictures of us kissing on Facebook and my grandpa saw the ring. I can't bring home a different person."

He grinned. "I'd be lying if I told you I love when you say you need me, but we have one big problem. Bigger than the ring and the picture on Faccbook."

She placed her hands on her hips. "And what would that be?"

"You want me to be convincing, right?"

"That's what I said."

"Well, the truth is, if I had a fiancée I would worship the ground she walked on. She would get all the love and respect and attention in the world from me. I would put my fiancée above all things in my life. I would give her everything I've got. *Every*thing. And that includes lovin', touchin', and squeezin', for starters." He took a step closer to Amy. "Your family will know I would be a dead man walkin' without you. They'll have no doubts that I can't live without you. And they sure as hell would know I'd honor and cherish and protect you because *you* are the best thing that ever happened to me . . . I mean, *if* you were my fiancée."

Amy swallowed hard.

It was possible she had slipped into a standing coma.

She did that staring thing again, too.

Luke snapped his fingers in front of her face.

Nothing.

"And one more thing," he said.

Amy hesitated, but then opened her mouth. "Yes?"

"I'm driving."

CHAPTER FIVE

Amy sat at the kitchen table waiting for Luke. She'd told him to pick her up at three in the afternoon and it was two minutes until the top of the hour. Thoughts of the romantic things he'd said last night popped into her head.

They will know I can't live without you. And they sure as hell would know I'd honor and cherish and protect you because you are the best thing that ever happened to me.

Nathan had never said anything like that.

No man in her life had ever said anything even close.

The ring of the doorbell made her jump, snapping her out of swooning.

She needed to focus.

He was her fake fiancé.

This was business.

Amy opened the front door and froze.

Luke was registering high on her hunk-o-meter, standing in front of her in his unwrinkled red and black plaid flannel shirt and Wranglers. She thought of what Jennie had said when they had seen Luke for the first time at the Double Deuce.

My-oh-my-oh-my.

Luke tipped his hat. "Good afternoon, ma'am. You ready?"

She nodded. "Ready, cowboy." She reached for her suitcase and—

"I've got it." Luke stepped in front of her and grabbed the suitcase by the handle.

Before she could object he was already halfway down the driveway, heading to his truck on the street. He lugged the suitcase instead of using the wheels. Not an easy feat, considering how much that thing weighed. Luckily, he didn't ask why it weighed so much.

He placed her suitcase next to his on the backseat of the extended cab, shut the door, and then opened the passenger door for her. "Your chariot awaits you, m'lady."

"Thank you," Amy said, trying to curtsy, losing her balance, and almost falling over.

Luke reached out and caught her, tilting her back upright.

"You didn't see that," Amy said.

"The only thing I see is a beautiful woman."

She stepped up into the truck and slid onto the leather seat. "And I already told you to knock off the charm because it won't work on me."

"Won't work? Then why did you fasten your seatbelt into my buckle?"

Horrified, Amy glanced down at her seatbelt.

She gritted her teeth.

It was fastened exactly where it was supposed to be fastened.

In her buckle.

Luke's grin was so wide it must have reached the back of his head. "Gotcha." He winked at Amy, then shut her door.

She decided not to check out Luke's butt this time, which was a good thing, since he glanced through the windshield at her as he worked his way around the front of the truck.

Once inside the truck he slid the key in the ignition. "We don't have a lot of time, so we should use the drive over there to get to know each other. You want me to be convincing, so I need to learn intimate things about you that a fiancé would know. Things like your job. Your hobbies. And how we met, for starters."

Amy nodded, glad to see he was all-in and taking this seriously. "You're right. And there are things you need to know about my family."

He grinned and started the engine. "If they're anything like you, this should be fun."

The ride to Julian from San Diego would be short, about an hour and fifteen minutes depending on traffic, so that didn't give them much time to get to know each other.

Luke pulled onto the highway and shot Amy a quick glance. "Okay, how do you want to do this?"

"How about if I tell you some things about me and then you can tell me some things about you?" Amy said. "Then we can fill in the blanks."

"Good plan. Go for it."

"Okay," she said, thinking where she should start. "I was born and raised in Julian. I moved to San Diego to study at the San Diego Culinary Institute. Got my first job a week after I graduated, one thing led to another, and now I'm a pastry chef at the Marriott Marquis and Marina down by the water."

"Impressive," Luke said.

She sighed. "I guess so. I make assembly-line desserts for corporate events and tourists I will most likely never see again."

"Is there anything you like about your job?"

She thought about it. "The end of the day." She laughed. "Seriously, it's not so bad. The hotel treats their employees very well. But after I clock out I leave with a box or two of leftover desserts that I made. I drop them off at an assisted living place or homeless shelter on the way home. Doing that makes me feel good about my job. Other than that, I'm not so sure."

"You had higher aspirations?"

Amy nodded. "Much higher, but my dad wanted me to stay in Julian and work on the family farm."

"And your mom?"

"She died."

"I'm so sorry," Luke said, reaching over and squeezing her hand.

"Thanks. Lucky for me, Aunt Barbara—my dad's sister—has always been around. She's almost been like a mom to me. She lives with my dad and my grandparents on the farm, along with Ruben our ranch hand. My dad is hard-headed and Aunt Barbara's just about the only person who can talk sense into him, although not always. She's a hoot—you'll love her. She used to be a nun, but now she does the marketing for our pie company, and also sells essential oils on the side."

Luke shot a glance in Amy's direction and then got his eyes back on the road. "Seriously?"

She laughed. "Seriously. She's something—you'll see. She's one of the most authentic people you'll ever meet. She tells it like it is and won't hesitate to call someone on their bullshit."

He smiled. "I like her already. Do you have any siblings?"

Amy nodded. "Just one. My brother Rod, Jennie's dad. He's divorced and lives in Maui. He teaches high school and surfs every afternoon when he gets off work. Rough life."

Luke chuckled. "Not a bad way to live at all. Tell me more about the farm and the pie company. Why aren't you involved in any of the operations?"

Amy sighed. "That's a long story."

He grinned. "I've got a week."

"We have over two thousand apple trees on the property and we make amazing pies, but as for why I'm not involved . . . I don't know."

"Really?"

Amy shrugged. "Okay, maybe I do. I guess I wanted more than something that was handed to me by my family. Plus, my dad isn't the easiest person in the world to be around. Especially after my mom died. Maybe if he retired . . . Anyway, I wanted to prove I could do something on my own. I wanted my own business."

"So, why did you give up on your dream?" Luke asked.

That was a harsh question. Had she given up or just pushed her dream to the side?

"I'm not sure I ever made a conscious decision to quit pursuing it at some point," Amy said. "It just happened. *Life* happened. I have a secure job and I guess I liked the idea of a life that was predictable."

"Safe."

Amy nodded. "Nothing wrong with that, is there?"

"Didn't say that there was, although sometimes it can be rewarding when you step outside your comfort zone."

"Most people aren't willing to take a chance with something new when they're my age."

"And what age might that be?"

Amy huffed. "That *might be* none of your business."

Luke chuckled. "So, you're saying I shouldn't know my fiancée's age? Hmmm. That's not realistic at all."

He had a good point. Amy's husband-to-be would know her age, but why did she feel weird telling him? Was she embarrassed? Why would she be? Maybe because society says forty-five-year-old women should be married, some already working on their second marriage.

"I'm thirty-five, if that makes you feel better," Luke said.

"I'm not telling you now."

He chuckled. "I think older women are sexy as hell. You know, in case you're older." He glanced over and winked.

"I'm forty-five," she blurted out.

She wanted to cover her face with her hands. Where had that come from? Why would she want Luke to think she was sexy?

"You look amazing," Luke said, grinning and switching lanes as they drove up Highway 67 past Dos Picos County Park. He glanced over to her again. "You should own that. You're a *very* attractive woman."

"Knock it off."

"Say *thank you* for once."

"Thank you." Amy paused a beat. "And knock it off."

They shared a laugh.

"But even if you looked your age or older than your age, it wouldn't matter," Luke said. "Your age doesn't define who you are. Your outlook on life does. Your attitude. And your actions."

"I'm on my way home to see the family and lie to them about having a fiancé. What does that say about me now?"

"I'll tell you what it says about you," Luke said. "You care. You don't want your father and grandparents to worry about you. This will make them feel better. You want your ex to move on, which means he'll find someone new. Plus, you donate food to nursing homes and homeless shelters. Your actions speak for themselves. But like I said at the Double Deuce, you're my type, but I have no interest in dating at this moment in my life."

"You keep saying that."

"It's the truth."

"Not that I'm interested at all either, but why are you so dead-set against dating?"

He waved a finger at Amy. "Not gonna go there."

"Why not?"

"Because that's not relevant since *we* are engaged to be married, my love."

She laughed before she could stop herself. "You're good. I have a whole week. I'll get it out of you."

"You're probably right," Luke said.

Amy smiled. "Okay, so let's move on to you, for now. The most important thing to keep in mind when we're on the farm is that you need to be one-hundred percent pure cowboy, through and through. Can you handle that?"

"That's all I *can* be, and that's why you pay me the big bucks."

"I can't believe I forgot this . . . can you ride a horse?"

Luke raised an eyebrow and gave her an *are you serious?* look.

"Of course, you can. If you can ride a bull, you should be able to ride a horse. Okay . . . do you know much about chickens and goats?"

Luke smirked. "I can tell them apart."

Amy's questions were getting dumber by the minute, but she was nervous and needed to settle down. Luke seemed to be the most confident man she'd ever met, so why was she worried? And why was she on the verge of freaking out? He needed to know what this meant to her.

"I'm not sure you understand what's on the line here," Amy said. "How important it is to me. I get anxious about going home."

"Huh . . . I'm not an expert, but it doesn't sound like you wanted to prove you could do something on your own at all. Sounds like you were trying to escape."

Amy opened her mouth and closed it.

"Sorry," Luke said. "I shouldn't be playing psychologist here. You have your reasons and it's none of my business."

"No. You may be right. I miss going home, but I want to pull my hair out when I think about visiting. It's because of my dad. He does this to me, which is sad, because I'm forty-five years old." She sighed. "I want to get through this and have Nathan out of my life."

"Relax," Luke said, reaching over and placing his hand on top of hers. "That's what's going to happen. I promise you. I won't let you down. I'll do whatever you want me to do. You can even boss me around. Tell me to giddy-up and I'll giddy-up."

She couldn't help but let out a little smile. "Okay." She nodded. "Okay."

He seemed to have the heart of a cowboy. Maybe he was a Western movie buff. Either that or he did a lot of research on cowboys for one of his acting roles. It didn't matter. What mattered was that she needed to learn more about his personal life so they didn't look like strangers when they were together in front of the family.

"Tell me some things," Amy said. "What do you like to do in your spare time? Do you have any hobbies? Any passions?"

"Barbecuing."

"Barbecuing?"

"That's right."

"Huh . . . I don't think anyone has ever told me that before. Well, you'll fit right in with my family because everything we do is centered around food. So, how good are you on the grill?"

"I'm not one to brag, but I've won a few national contests. I've been on television a couple of times, too. I only bring it up because it's something you should know about me, in case one of your family members have seen me on TV."

This wasn't much of a surprise. Luke was acting in a show at the Hillcrest Theater, and most actors had dreams of appearing on television and in the movies. This situation was unique because he could combine his love of acting and his love of barbecuing. Smart move on his part.

"What shows have you been on?" Amy asked.

"You ever heard of the show *Barbecue Pitmasters*?"

"Isn't that a reality TV show?"

"Sure is. I appeared on the 'When Pigs Fly' episode in season five."

Amy laughed. "You're serious?"

"Yup. Spent a week in Florida cookin' up spareribs and pork butt at the Smokin' in the Square festival. Helluva time and I won the whole darn thing."

Luke was a reality TV star? She never would have guessed it. Not that she was impressed because she'd never been a fan of reality TV. Amy preferred stories that tugged at the heart-strings, and romances where the man and woman lived happily ever after. She'd keep that to herself, since he was a man and probably preferred *Thor* and Jason Bourne movies.

"So, you got your fifteen minutes of fame?" Amy asked.

"Nah. I don't care about that."

"Oh . . ." She studied him for a moment. "You did it for the money?"

"I won a hundred grand but I didn't do it for the paycheck, either."

"Why did you do it then?"

"I love barbecuing," Luke said. "It's as simple as that."

"Well, sounds like you know your stuff."

"Thanks, but I need to give credit where credit is due. My grandpa taught me just about everything I know. Fish or beef or chicken or vegetables, you name it. I can cook ribs a hundred different ways."

"I had no idea there were so many options with the barbecue."

"You'd be surprised. You've got different barbecue styles all around the country . . . California, Texas, Memphis, Kansas City, the Carolinas. Different meat, different sauce or rub, different wood to burn. Even different types of grills. One burner. Two burners. Three. Four. Gas. Charcoal. Electric. Open grill. Covered. Vessel. Smoker. Rotisserie. Sorry. I told you it's my passion, but I get carried away sometimes."

Amy loved the way Luke's face lit up when he talked about barbecuing. He wasn't lying when he said he was passionate about it. That's how she used to be when she talked about desserts and pastries.

Used to be.

When was the last time she had felt that excitement about her career? That thrill of creating something new?

Too long ago, no doubt about that.

"Is this one of those cases where the student became better than the teacher?" Amy asked.

"No way. My grandparents are no longer around, but Grandpa was a true master of the grill. I couldn't hold a spatula to him. A good man, too. You would've loved him. Hell, he would've loved you."

The proud smile on Luke's face was endearing.

"Let me cook for you," he said.

That came out of nowhere and she had to admit it surprised her.

She didn't know how to respond.

"What?" Luke added. "You don't like to eat? I know you like to drink."

She playfully poked him on the arm. "Watch it."

"I still want to cook for you. You like burgers?"

"Love them."

"Good. I can fix up a burger that'll knock your socks off. You like beef?"

"If it came from a cow or a pig, I'll eat it."

"Cheese?"

"Yes, although that technically came from a cow, so you should already know the answer."

Luke nodded. "Good point. Avocado? Do they come from cows? No—they don't. Sorry, got confused there for a second."

"Are you making fun of me?"

Luke chuckled. "A little."

"Well, yes, I do love avocados. And I can eat anything. I'm

the least picky eater you'll ever meet. Spicy. Not spicy. Doesn't matter."

"Then it's settled," Luke said. "I will make you the best burger you've ever tasted. A quarter pound of fresh Angus beef, cheese, bacon, homemade chipotle sauce with a little zing, and avocado. Oh, let's add some sautéed onions for the heck of it."

"That sounds amazing."

"Good. You got it. Then I'll serve it on a lightly toasted bun, but not before I add one last ingredient."

"Which is?" Amy asked.

"A fried egg."

"You're kidding."

"Hey—I don't yolk about burgers."

She laughed and gestured to the extended cab. "Please tell me you have a barbecue in the back somewhere. I don't mind you pulling over to make it for me."

"Sorry." Luke chuckled and checked the imaginary shirt pocket on his chest with one hand. "I'm fresh out of eggs, too. I usually carry a few on me, just in case. You never know."

Amy laughed and pointed out the window to the Demler Brothers Egg Ranch sign on the side of the road. "There you go. They've got the best eggs. And their eggs have two yolks."

"No way," Luke said, yanking the steering wheel to the right, and pulling the truck off the road.

Amy held on as the truck slid sideways on the gravel, coming to a perfect, complete stop right in front of the door of the egg shack. "What are you doing? I was kidding."

"I need me some of them two-yolk eggs and I need 'em now. Be right back."

Luke got out of the truck and entered Demler Brothers, as

Amy sat there on the passenger side of his truck, her mouth hanging open.

She was shocked that Luke had stopped to buy eggs.

Shocked that she felt so alive when she was around him

Shocked that she suddenly looked forward to spending the week with him.

CHAPTER SIX

Luke paid for the flat of eggs and pushed the door open with the side of his shoulder to head back to the truck. He glanced up at Amy staring back at him through the windshield. He'd told her he had no interest in dating at this moment in his life, but it would be hard to resist a woman like her. He wasn't lying when he also told her he'd put his woman above all things in his life. And that was the exact reason why he couldn't be seeing anyone, including her. How could he give her everything when he couldn't even figure out his own life? His own career? Which was sad because there was nothing better than having a woman in his life. But that woman would have to wait until he got his career back on track.

After sliding the flat of eggs into the back of the extended cab, Luke hopped back in and smiled at Amy before pulling the truck back onto the road.

Amy gestured back to the extended cab with her thumb. "I can't believe you bought a whole flat of eggs."

"Super jumbo. Hey—you only live once."

She laughed. "And you want to live it up with eggs, do ya?"

"Two-*yolk* eggs. You said your family revolves around food." He grinned and then pointed to a sign that said *Entering Historic Julian District. Historical Landmark No. 412.* "That was fast. We're here."

"Almost," Amy said. "We need to go through town and pass a few wineries. Six minutes without stops or stopping for tourists darting across the road."

Luke drove up the main road in the center of town, admiring the shops and restaurants on both sides, many of them with a sign on the door or window that said *Pies*.

"You weren't kidding about this place being known for pies," Luke said. "Pies on every corner. We should stop for a slice."

"Not a good idea."

"You only live once," Luke said, pulling over.

"You sound like my Grandpa Leo. And something tells me I'll be hearing it all week long."

"Not a bad motto to have."

"No. It's not, but we're not going to eat dessert before dinner. My family likes to eat early, so the food will be on the table at five on the dot." She pointed to the clock on the dashboard console. "That's less than an hour from now. Plus, our family makes our own pies, remember?"

Luke glanced out the window at the Julian Pie Company. "And because of that you'll never eat other people's pies?"

"Something like that."

Luke stared at her. "You're kidding, right? Have you at least been inside one of these places?"

Amy didn't answer.

"Tell me you say hello when you see the owners or an employee on the street."

She grimaced. "We cross to the other side of the street if we see someone coming in our direction to avoid any awkward situations."

Wow.

"This must be some serious rivalry," Luke said, pulling over.

"A friendly rivalry," she corrected.

"Doesn't sound so friendly if you're scared to talk with them or go inside."

"I'm *not* scared."

"Then let's go." Luke winked and jumped out of the truck, closing the door before she could protest. Amy didn't move a muscle, keeping her butt planted in the passenger seat. She stared at Luke through the windshield with the same look she'd given him right before she had poked him in the chest at the Double Deuce. Then she sighed and mouthed a firm *no*, waving him back inside the truck.

Luke opened the door of the truck and leaned in across the seat. "Yes, my love?" He looked through the windshield at the pie shop and then back at Amy. "What seems to be the problem?"

"Okay . . . There's an unwritten, unspoken rule in our family. We don't eat their pies, okay?" She gestured up the street. "There's another popular place a few doors up. Mom's Pies. We don't eat their pies, either."

"Aren't you even curious?" Luke asked.

"Of course I'm curious! I'm a pastry chef and can appreciate creations from other people. I'm not so egotistical to think our pies are the only good pies in the world. And I see the lines going out the doors for both places and the reviews online, so they know what they're doing. I'll admit I've even dreamed of going in there and tasting each pie, one by one, and trying to figure out the exact ingredients they used."

"That sounds like fun. Count me in."

Amy sighed. "I can't. I don't want to upset my dad or my grandparents."

He pointed to her face and grinned. "See that? I told you you're as sweet as sugar. In fact, that's your new nickname. Sugar." He jumped back in the truck. "And I love pie, so we *will* be back at some point this week."

"No. We won't."

"Yes. We will."

"We'll have plenty of pie at home."

"Not that I doubt it, but what makes your pies so special?"

Amy thought about it for a moment. "Believe it or not, like your barbecuing the secret is usually in the spices. And since you're going to cook me a burger, I'll bake you a pie." She smiled and he felt his heart thump. "Maybe."

"Well, well." Luke studied her for a moment. "Look at you."

"What?" Amy said.

"I don't know. It almost feels like you're being *nice*."

"Hey—I can be nice. I need to watch out for you."

"Why?" Luke said. "What did I do?"

"It's what you didn't do."

"Okay. What didn't I do?"

Amy waved a finger at him. "Nope. Not gonna go there." She crossed her arms. "Not relevant since *we* are engaged to be married, *my love*."

Luke laughed. "Good one. By the way, I want to bring

something else. All we have are eggs so far. Since you've banned pies, what about flowers? Are those off-limits, too?"

She smiled. "No. They aren't necessary, but flowers are fine and a lovely gesture on your part." She pointed across the street to Flowers by Lani. "There you go. Knock yourself out."

Luke bought three bouquets of flowers and then made one more stop at Menghini Winery to pick up a couple of bottles of wine. A minute later, they drove up the long driveway to Amy's family's farmhouse. It was a large property with hundreds of apple trees on both sides of the driveway.

"What an amazing place," Luke said, checking out the horse stable and giant green barn.

"Yeah," she said, sighing. "There's no place like home."

And what a home it was.

"How many bedrooms do you have in this place?"

Amy stared out the window. "Six." She pointed. "Plus, a guest house over there and a cottage for Ruben, the ranch hand, over there."

As they got closer to the house, Luke eyed all the cars parked on both sides of the driveway. "Looks like you've got one mighty big family."

"Not *that* big," Amy said. "Something is going on, and I don't have a good feeling about this."

Amy told Luke to park on the left side of the barn. They left their suitcases and eggs in the cab of the truck and would come back for them later, opting to carry in the flowers and wine.

They walked to the front door and paused on the step.

For so many cars on the property, it sure was quiet. Maybe everyone had walked over to the hot springs for a dip. The property sat on forty acres with a secluded hot springs, one of her favorite places to relax and unwind.

"Ready, Freddy?" Amy asked, grabbing the front door handle.

"Ready, spaghetti," Luke said, removing his hat.

Amy turned the handle and pushed open the front door.

They both stepped inside and froze.

"Surprise!" a whole slew of people yelled, popping up from behind the furniture.

There must have been fifteen, maybe eighteen of them. Phones were held in the air, people taking pictures and recording video.

None of their eyes were on Amy.

Luke had been there for ten seconds and he already felt like he was being put under a microscope, like a tick from the ass of one of those beautiful horses outside.

Amy glanced around the room, the smile on her face not at all convincing. "What's going on?" She rocked back and forth from one leg to the other.

An older man stepped forward, most likely her Grandpa Leo.

"It's all for you, my little sweetie pie," he said. "We wanted to throw you an engagement party."

Amy's face turned whiter than her silk blouse, and Luke knew why since he'd been to an engagement party a few months ago. Stories would be shared. Drinks would be flowing. Gifts would be given. And embarrassing games would most certainly be played.

There would be plenty of opportunities for one of them to slip up.

Luke and Amy were supposed to get to know each other

more in the car, but it was such a short ride it hadn't happened. And then they got distracted with the eggs and the pie shops and the flowers. He only knew three main things about her, other than the ranch and the apple pies.

She was pretty as hell. She was sweet as sugar. She was a pastry chef.

Oh—there was one other thing he knew.

They were in a heap of trouble.

CHAPTER SEVEN

"An engagement party?" Amy said, trying with all her might to keep the horrified feeling she had in her stomach from registering on her face. She needed to remain calm. But how could she remain calm when she and Luke had been thrown into the lion's den with bloody steaks tied around their necks? And they'd just walked in the door!

Not good at all.

"You shouldn't have done this," Amy said, wishing she had the power to snap her fingers and make everyone disappear. "This week is all about Grandpa Leo."

"Nonsense," Grandpa Leo said. "Your engagement is much bigger news than me turning ninety. Besides, I'm going to live until I'm two-hundred years old, so I haven't even had my mid-life crisis yet."

"Now, don't just stand there," Grams said. "Introduce us to that good-looking man."

Luke grabbed Amy's hand, squeezing it.

Amy hesitated and forced a smile. "Everyone, this is . . .

Luke Jenkins, my . . ." Amy's heart rate went up, but she was unsure if it was because of the deception that was now in play with her family or because Luke was holding her hand.

Definitely the hand-holding.

Luke let go of her hand and wrapped his arm around Amy, pulling her closer and smiling. "Her fiancé. Thanks so much for having me." He pulled her closer, if that was possible.

Amy nodded and forced a smile as she patted his chest. "Yup. My fiancé."

She glanced around the room at her dad, her aunt Barbara, her grandparents, her childhood friend Dawn with her husband Curtis, and a few cousins and longtime neighbors.

Jennie was there, too, but with a man who wasn't her ex. Amy had yet to have a chat with her niece since she'd taken that scandalous photo and posted it on Facebook. Okay, maybe *scandalous* was the wrong word, but the photo looked like it was taken by the paparazzi. The angle of the shot made it look like Amy was trying to devour Luke's entire face during their kiss. Jennie had a bright future ahead of her working for the tabloids.

Aunt Barbara stepped forward, smiling and holding out her hand. "Such a pleasure to meet you."

Instead of shaking Barbara's hand, Luke turned it palm-down and kissed the top, then offered her one of the bouquets. "A pleasure to meet you, ma'am."

"Well, aren't you the sweetest thing?" Barbara said, handing the flowers over to Amy's dad, Greg. "And please, call me Aunt Barbara."

"Will do, ma'am," Luke said.

"Aunt Barbara."

Luke smiled. "Aunt Barbara."

She pulled his hand closer to inspect it. "Your hands are a little dry, young man. I've got some oil that'll whip 'em into shape." She pulled a small bottle from the pouch around her waist, opened it, drizzled a few drops on his hand and rubbed. "Some rosewood, some jasmine, some avocado, and a special ingredient." She gave him his hand back. "There you go. Good as new. Feel it, feel it."

Luke rubbed his hand and nodded. "Nice."

"If you like that I've got some oil that'll—"

Amy cleared her throat. "Aunt Barbara, please."

"What?"

"Give the man a chance to settle in before pushing your products on him."

Aunt Barbara grabbed Luke's hand and squeezed it. "Don't listen to her. I'm not pushing anything on you. I've got free samples. Anyway, these oils sell themselves."

Luke winked. "I'm sure they do and I can't wait to try them, ma 'am." He grinned. "Aunt Barbara."

Amy gestured to her dad. "Luke, this is my dad, Greg."

Luke extended his smooth hand. "A pleasure to meet you, sir."

Her dad glanced down at Luke's hand before accepting it. He squeezed it so hard he was grinding his teeth, which was a joke because Amy was sure Luke could snap her dad in two with his thumb and index finger.

"Please. Call me Mr. Weaver," her dad said, still squeezing Luke's hand.

"Greg Weaver!" Barbara said. "You behave. He'll do no such thing. Luke, you can call him Greg or Mr. Stubborn, like I call him."

"I was kidding!" Greg said.

He wasn't kidding.

Still, Amy loved how Luke handled it. He wasn't flustered by her dad's rudeness.

"This is my grandmother, Betty," Amy said, preferring to move on and get through everyone.

Luke handed the second bouquet to Amy's grandmother and kissed her on the top of the hand. "Pleased to meet you, ma'am."

Grandma Betty waved him off. "You're such a kind young man, but we're family here. You don't have to ma'am me. You can *Gram* me. Call me Grams."

"Yes, ma'am. I mean . . . Grams."

Everyone laughed, including Amy, who pointed to the last bouquet in Luke's hands. "Who are those for?"

Luke winked. "They're for you, my love." He handed her the bouquet and kissed her on the cheek. "They're not as pretty as my fiancée, but they smell almost as nice."

Amy cheeks were burning up. "Thank you."

"That man is a keeper!" Grams said, turning to Grandpa Leo. "How come you don't give me flowers anymore?"

"Because the flowers always get so dang jealous of your beauty. Poor things." Grandpa Leo winked and kissed her on the lips. Then he turned Luke and fist-bumped him. "I still got it."

"That you do," Luke said, chuckling. "I'm taking notes."

"We men have to treasure our ladies. Treat 'em like queens."

"I agree, sir," Luke said. "You only live once."

"My sentiments exactly!" Grandpa Leo said, fist-bumping Luke again.

That was the craziest thing Amy had ever seen.

Grandpa fist-bumped Luke.

Since when did her grandpa fist-bump anyone? He was ninety, for goodness sake, not a high school teenager.

After the rest of the introductions, Grandpa Leo put his arm around Luke's shoulder and ushered him toward the booze on the other side of the room. They looked like they were already best friends.

"Where are you taking him?" Amy asked, feeling anxious. She and Luke needed to stick together at all times.

"Gotta get this fine man a drink," Grandpa Leo said, not turning back.

Amy couldn't let Luke out of her sight. Not even for a minute. In fact, it would be best if she took him back out to the car to get their suitcases. While they were there she would use the time to get their stories straight. They never discussed where they had met, how he had proposed, and at what stage of the wedding planning they were in. Did they even have a wedding date yet?

Amy darted across the room after Luke, but Dawn cut her off.

"This once-a-year crap isn't working for me," Dawn said, pulling Amy into a hug. "Seriously, you need to visit more, or move back and work here with your family again."

Amy pulled away from her good friend's hug. "Don't you start. I'm expecting plenty of that from my dad."

"Fine, but you've been holding back on me," Dawn said. "How come you didn't mention you were seeing someone the last time we talked on the phone?"

"Well . . ."

"More than *seeing* someone, you're getting married! Geez

Louise, you know how to pick 'em. He looks like one of them Hollywood actors."

If you only knew.

"Where did you meet him?" Dawn asked.

The questions had already begun, and Amy didn't have an answer.

"Um . . ." Amy said, glancing over to the other side of the room at Luke while stalling for time. "You'll have to wait to find out."

Dawn arched an eyebrow. "Why is that?"

"Because," Amy said, dragging it out as long as she could because lying was much, much harder than she ever imagined. "Luke and I want to tell the story to everyone at the same time. During dinner."

Dawn studied her. "What's going on? You look nervous."

"Nothing's going on!" Amy said, louder than she had planned.

"Well, can I at least see the ring?"

"*That* you can," Amy said, holding her hand up, but then realizing that Dawn had seen Jennie's engagement ring before. She crossed her fingers that her best friend wouldn't notice how similar they were. or that they were actually the same ring.

"It's beautiful." Dawn said, pulling Amy's hand closer and inspecting the ring from top to bottom. "Why does this seem so familiar?"

"Did I already show you?"

"No—you didn't."

"It's a popular style." Amy yanked her hand back. "I have to do something. I'll be right back."

"But . . ."

Amy weaved in and out of everyone avoiding eye contact, so she wouldn't have to stop and talk to someone else. She needed to get to Luke. They needed to talk.

Too bad she never made it.

Bad luck struck again as Amy's dad pulled her into a hug. "Glad you found time for your family."

"I'm busy with my career," Amy said, glancing over toward Luke.

Her dad followed her gaze. "I see. So, if your career is taking up so much of your time, how is it you could land yourself a fiancé?"

Amy swallowed hard. "Love just happens. It's unpredictable."

"Uh-huh," he said, not sounding convinced at all. "Well, the man is not off to a good start, I'll tell you that much. He didn't have the decency of asking my permission to marry you."

"Are you aware what year it is, Dad? I'm forty-five years old. You don't have to approve of the person I marry although I hope you would assume I would make a good choice. I can take care of myself."

"Nathan took me out to dinner to tell me about his intentions to marry you and ask for my blessing," he said, ignoring what Amy had said. "There's still time to reconsider. He's a catch."

Her dad was already talking about her ex again. That didn't take long. Amy knew her dad would start pushing Nathan on her, but she didn't think he would still do it while she was engaged to another man.

Well, *fake*-engaged, but still . . .

She had no feelings for Nathan.

"That's a sign of respect," he continued, not taking Amy's eye roll as a hint to stuff a sock in it. "In fact, I always know what to expect from Nathan. He comes from a good, hard-working family." He glanced over toward Luke again. "And what does Luke do for a living?"

Why did it matter? She should've known her dad would grill her. And she needed to say something fast before he got even more suspicious.

"He . . ."

What does he do?

Crap.

She couldn't tell her dad he was an actor because her dad would laugh. She couldn't say he barbecued either, could she? She hated that she cared what her dad thought. Not that Amy disapproved of being an actor or someone who barbecued, but that would get her dad going on having a secure, responsible job. Amy and Luke agreed he would play the part of a cowboy, but what type of cowboy? Was he on the pro-rodeo circuit? Did he tend to the cattle on the ranch? Did he *own* a ranch?

"Hold that thought, Dad," Amy said, choosing to flee the scene than rather come up with an answer. "I'll be right back."

"Where are you going?"

Amy pretended she didn't hear her dad and wove through a few more people before getting to Luke, who was already talking about barbecuing with Grandpa Leo.

"You roasted a whole pig?" Grandpa Leo said. "I hear that's difficult. They do them in Hawaii at those fancy luaus at the hotels, although they roast them in the ground over there."

"I've done that, too," Luke said. "I can grill anything, but my specialty is Memphis-style smoked spareribs and Texas-style beef brisket."

"Sounds tasty."

"I'd be happy to make it for you one day."

"I might take you up on that," Grandpa Leo said, clinking beer bottles with Luke.

Amy cleared her throat. "Luke? Can I talk to you for a minute?"

Luke turned and smiled. "You can, sugar." He reached out and pulled Amy against him, wrapping his arms around her. "Did you miss me already?"

"With every fiber of my being."

"That's my girl," Luke said. "Let me get you a drink."

Amy gestured toward the door. "In a minute. Can we talk? Please? It's important."

"Now, where are you two off to?" Grandpa Leo asked. "You can't leave your own engagement party."

"Just for a moment." Amy hesitated. "We . . . need to get our suitcases out of Luke's truck. Plus, he bought eggs from Demler Brothers for us."

"Two-yolk eggs!" Grandpa Leo said. "Love those suckers. So fresh and tasty."

Grams approached. "That is so sweet of you, Luke. Just for that I'll make you the best omelet in the morning."

"That's mighty kind of you, ma'am," Luke said.

She wagged her finger at him. "What did I tell you earlier?"

He smiled. "That's very kind of you, *Grams*, but you don't need to go to any trouble."

"It's no trouble at all."

"Anyway, you don't need to worry about your stuff," Grandpa Leo said. "Ruben already got everything from your truck. The eggs are in the kitchen and your suitcases are already in the guesthouse." He turned to Luke. "Ruben is our ranch hand. You'll see him around. He's been with the family for over forty years."

"Why did you take our suitcases to the guesthouse?" Amy asked, not at all interested in talking about Ruben, even though they were close.

Amy loved the guesthouse, but it had one king-sized problem. The bed.

One bed.

There was no way she was sleeping in the same bed with Luke.

Or the same room.

"Where else are you and Luke going to sleep?" Grandpa Leo said. "You could use a little time alone and you won't get that in the main house." He winked.

"Ain't that the truth," Grams said. "You'll have all the privacy in the world if you want to run around naked and—"

"Grams!" Amy said.

"What? I'm just keeping it real, as you young kids say."

Young kids? Amy was forty-five years old. And even if she wanted to keep it real, she wouldn't be keeping it real with Luke.

Grandpa Leo fist-bumped Luke again for the third time.

Then the two clinked beer bottles.

What in the heck is going on here?

"I've got some wonderful essential oils that you can use later in your room, if you know what I mean," Aunt Barbara said, fishing around in her oil pouch. "It's here somewhere. I call them intimacy oils."

Amy sighed. "Thanks, but no thanks."

"It's a special mix of fennel, rose, sandalwood, and—"

"Aunt Barbara, please."

"What? A little dab will do ya and you'll be good to go. All. Night. Long."

Amy crossed her arms.

"Oh. I get it. No issues in that department." Aunt Barbara eyed Luke up and down. "Not a surprise. Such a strong, strong man." She squeezed Luke's arm and then turned her attention back to Amy. "But I do need to give you something to help you loosen up."

"Not. Necessary."

Aunt Barbara winked. "I think it is. I'm expecting another calming oil shipment soon that's a mix of ylang ylang and pig pheromones. It'll calm you down and pump you up at the same time!" She turned toward the door. "I think the delivery is here."

Things were spiraling out of control, and Amy and Luke had barely been there thirty minutes. Plus, she was starving. Why didn't she smell anything cooking? The family was always punctual with meals, so it made little sense since it was five.

Five was always mealtime.

"Pizza is here." Barbara returned, a pizza delivery man following behind with a tall stack of pizza boxes. She pointed to the counter. "Put them over there. Okay everyone, come and get it while it's hot."

At least there was one thing going right. Supper was right on time. And Amy didn't need any of those fancy oils to calm down. The pizza would do the trick.

Luke and Amy grabbed paper plates and a couple of slices of pizza from one of the pizza boxes on the island counter. They were about to sit at one of the temporary folding tables off to the side of the kitchen when they were waved over by

Grams standing by the long, rustic farm table made from reclaimed wood.

The one right in the middle of the kitchen.

Grams patted the spot on the table in between two place-mats. "Luke and Amy, we have your reserved places here since you're the guests of honor. This is so exciting."

"Thank you," Luke said, sliding onto the bench next to Amy.

Greg slid onto the bench across from Luke and gave him the stare-down.

Amy couldn't believe what she was seeing. Her dad had turned into Robert De Niro from the movie *Meet the Parents*. If he pulled out a lie-detector machine they were out of there.

"Luke," Greg said, not wasting any time. "Pardon us for not even knowing you existed."

"No problem at all, sir," Luke said, taking a bite of his pizza. "I can assure you that I do exist."

Everyone laughed except Amy's father.

Greg cleared his throat. "Yes, well, since we don't know squat about you, please enlighten us. Tell us what you do for a living, for starters."

Showtime.

Amy turned to Luke, curious how he would hold up under the pressure of her father. How he handled the first of what most likely would be many questions would be a tell-tale sign of how the rest of the week would go. All eyes in the kitchen were on Luke, which may not be intimidating to an actor, but Amy didn't like the uneasy feeling in her stomach.

Luke placed the pizza slice back down on his paper plate. "Well, sir, I'm a barbecue pitmaster."

Amy glanced back across the table to her dad for his reaction.

He had a blank look on his face.

"A barbecue what?" Greg said.

"Pitmaster."

"A barbecue pitmaster." Greg squished his eyebrows together. "So, what exactly *is* that? You clean barbecues for a living?"

Amy wouldn't have blamed Luke for laughing, but he kept a straight face.

"No, sir," Luke said. "I prepare the food. I'm a chef. Barbecuing is my passion."

"Your passion . . ." Greg stared at Luke. "So . . . you're *a cook.* There can't be much money in that, can there? How are you going to support my daughter?"

Amy didn't like the disdainful tone in her father's voice. How dare he?

"I don't need supporting, Dad," Amy said. "I can take care of—"

Greg held up his hand to cut her off. "I'm trying to get to know Luke. Please let the man answer the question."

"Sure," Luke said. "I guess you could call me a cook, since I'm cooking when I'm on the grill, but I'm known as a chef in most circles. As for the money, barbecuing is almost a three billion-dollar industry."

That got her dad's attention.

"And with all due respect, sir, Amy doesn't need to be taken care of. She's got an amazing career of her own as a pastry chef. I'm sure you're also well aware of how talented your daughter is."

Amy's eyes were back on her father's.

"Of course, but—"

"*Very* talented," Luke said, cutting off Greg and scoring huge points with Amy. "Yes, if something were to ever happen to her career, her life, anything at all, I could handle the responsibility. But all my money is on Amy taking the world by storm because she's one of the most determined women I've ever met. You taught her well, Mr. Weaver."

That was clever. Luke defended Amy, and then gave the credit to her dad. Her dad's ego was too big to not take the credit for that.

Luke was a genius.

The table was silent, waiting for Greg's response.

"Uh . . . thank you," Greg said, taking a sip of his beer and then grabbing a slice of pizza.

Amazing.

Luke had shut up her dad.

Nobody had ever shut him up.

That was worth a kiss!

Amy scratched that thought from her brain.

His kisses were unreal, but she wasn't going there.

Her dad was quiet, and that's what mattered. Well . . . quiet for the moment. Luke won the first round, but that wouldn't be the last from her dad on the subject.

Amy sighed and took another bite of her pizza.

You can pick your friends, but you can't pick your parents.

"How did you two meet?" Aunt Barbara asked.

"Yes," Jennie said, smiling. "Tell us."

Jennie knew darn well how they had met.

Luke turned to Amy. "Would you like to answer, sugar? Or shall I?"

Amy was terrified of sticking her foot in her mouth. Luke

handled himself well with the first round, so she opted to let him continue.

"You can tell them," Amy said. "Your version will be much better than mine, cowboy."

"It would be my pleasure," Luke said, leaning toward her.

What is he doing? Is he going to kiss me? He'd better not because—

Luke's lips were on Amy's before she could do a thing.

His soft, warm, lovely lips.

No tongue.

The kiss rendered her speechless.

Amy blinked.

What day is it?

Luke glanced down at her lips again and winked.

Amy snapped out of the kiss coma and she knew exactly what day it was.

This was the day Luke would die.

CHAPTER EIGHT

Amy would need a day planner to keep track of the people she had to kill this week. She had told Luke more than once that there would be no more kisses. Why did she even have rules if he wasn't going to obey them? Luke was taking advantage of the situation because everyone was watching them. He shouldn't have kissed her. Sure, she'd enjoyed it, but that had nothing to do with it.

"You've got yourself such a passionate man there," Grams said, turning to Grandpa Leo. "Kiss me like that."

"It would be a pleasure but remember that could cause my enlarged heart to explode out of my chest because your kisses are like dynamite." Grandpa Leo winked and leaned over, giving her a good smacker across the lips. "Okay, where were we?"

"They were going to tell us how they met," Dawn said.

"It's a funny story," Luke said, running his fingers through his hair, thinking. "Amy and I met at a wedding at the Marriott Marquis and Marina down by the water."

Amy turned to Luke and tried to keep her surprise under wraps, but she couldn't believe he remembered where she worked. She had only mentioned it one time. It was the perfect place for them to have met. Had she mentioned he was a genius?

"I love weddings!" Aunt Barbara said. "What a coincidence. You met at a wedding and now you're going to have one of your own. Don't tell me. Amy was the maid of honor and you were the best man? And she caught the bouquet. Is that how you met? I remember a movie like that. What was the name of that movie?"

"Would you let him finish?" Grams said.

"Sorry, Luke," Aunt Barbara said. "Please continue. But I still hope you were the best man."

Luke shook his head. "I wish it were more romantic than that, but we were both working at the wedding, not guests. Still, we could enjoy the event and appreciate the setting. It was out of this world."

"What was so special about it?" Grams asked.

"The wedding reception was outside on the Coronado Terrace, a private area by the water that has panoramic views of the San Diego Bay and Coronado Island. I was barbecuing tri-tip for the guests while Amy was setting up the wedding cake and desserts on a table near the dance area." He turned to Amy. "Do you remember what type of cake they had at that wedding, sugar?"

Why was he asking her? He was the one creating all this bullshit on the fly. He was the actor!

Amy hesitated, blindsided by the question. "Um . . . red velvet . . . I think."

Luke reached under the table and squeezed her hand. "That was it. Red velvet."

Wow, he was playing the part so well Amy almost believed him. Maybe she shouldn't be surprised. Most actors could improvise. Still, it was time for him to quit while he was ahead. Hopefully, the story wouldn't be long.

"Even in that white pastry chef uniform she had to wear when she worked for the hotel, Amy was as breathtaking as could be," Luke said. "I didn't think anyone could ever look good in a puffy white hat, but she pulled it off."

Puffy white hat? Okay, that was a bit of a stretch.

There was no puffy white hat!

Luke was getting a little carried away, and she had to reel him back in before he flubbed everything up.

"Thank you," Amy said. "You know how to tell the story well."

"It sounds like it was meant to be," Jennie said, giving Amy a knowing smile.

"It sure was. Anyway, now you all know our story. Can someone pass me another slice of the combination pizza? I have no idea why I'm so hungry."

Luke held up his hand. "Hold on, now, sugar. I haven't even gotten to the good part."

"Good part?" Amy said, reaching under the table and pinching Luke on the leg.

She should've known he wouldn't even flinch.

Damn him and those firm muscles.

"They don't want to hear any more," Amy pressed. "Can you pass the parmesan cheese and chili flakes this way, Dawn?"

"There's more to the story?" Grams asked. "Well, we need to hear it!"

"We do," Aunt Barbara said. "Tell us everything. What happened, Luke?"

"I'm glad you asked," Luke said. "But you won't believe it."

"What do you mean?" Grams said.

"Tell us," Grandpa Leo said, on the edge of his chair. "The suspense is not good for my dilated cardiomyopathy."

"Amy fell into the bay," Luke continued.

"No," Aunt Barbara said, putting both palms on her cheeks. "How did that happen?"

Amy jerked her head in Luke's direction, shocked he was taking it this far. The man was obsessed. But how could she stop him? All eyes were on Luke and he was giving the performance of a lifetime, but he needed to stop before he stuck his foot in his mouth or she had a nervous breakdown.

"I had to jump in the water to save her," Luke added.

"Luke," Amy whispered. "You can stop now. Please."

"Now, this is romantic!" Grandpa Leo said. "We've got a real live hero in our presence." He glanced over at Amy and cocked his head to the side. "How on earth did you fall in the water?"

Amy hesitated. "I . . . uh . . ."

"She was trying to save a duckling that got separated from its mother and the rest of the brood," Luke said, almost a little too cheerfully.

You have got to be kidding me.

A duckling? Come on, they would *never* believe—

*Aw*s filled the kitchen.

Okay, so the suckers had bought it.

Luke sat up in his chair. "She leaned over the chain to grab the duckling, but couldn't reach and splash! Into the water she went. Headfirst. The puffy white hat never made it. To the bottom of the bay it sank."

This nonsense had to stop.

"Honey," Amy said, patting Luke on the hand and still trying to stop him. "My love . . . I think that's enough for one evening."

Too bad he continued.

"Then a passing German barge carrying beer and BMWs to the Port of San Diego created a heavy undercurrent that pulled Amy and the little duckling out farther into the bay."

"Oh, no!" Grams said.

"Oh, *yes!*" Luke said. "I was just as shocked as you. I didn't know her but she would not die on my watch, no matter how ridiculous her puffy hat was."

"I thought her puffy white hat sank when she fell in?" Aunt Barbara said, arching an eyebrow.

She caught everything. Amy had warned Luke, but he hadn't listened.

Luke blinked. "It did sink. That's right. I mentioned it again, because it brings back memories. I *loved* that hat. Anyway, I left the tri-tip unattended on the barbecue and dove into the water to rescue Amy and the duckling. And that's it! We went on our first date a week later and the rest is history."

"That is the most amazing story!" Grandpa Leo said, lifting his beer bottle in the air. "A toast to Luke for saving Amy's life!"

"And the duckling!" Grams added.

Everyone except Amy's dad raised their drinks and called out together, "Cheers!"

Greg glared at Luke. "A German barge with beer and

BMWs, huh?"

"That's right, sir." Luke took a sip of his beer.

Greg didn't take his eyes off Luke as he took a long pull of his beer.

After dinner, Amy's dad came around to their side of the table and squatted down between Amy and Luke. "Something's going on with you two. I know it."

"Of course there's something going on," Amy said. "We're getting married."

Greg's glance shot back and forth between Luke and Amy. "So you say . . ." He turned to Luke. "BMW has a manufacturing plant in South Carolina. How do you suppose they got a barge from South Carolina to San Diego with all of that land in the middle?" He crossed his arms, waiting for an answer.

Luke didn't hesitate. "BMW has manufacturing plants all over the world, sir. I hear some limited-edition models are brought over from abroad, so that barge could have come from anywhere directly into San Diego. I can do research if it's something you need to know."

"No," Greg said, standing back up. "But I still think something fishy is going on here." More glances shot back and forth between Luke and Amy.

If her dad found out they were faking the engagement, Nathan would be the next to know, and then Amy would be back to square one.

This wasn't good at all.

Could things get any worse?

"Okay, everyone!" Dawn called out. "Grab your drinks and head to the family room. Leave the two chairs in the middle of the room for Luke and Amy. We're going to play *How Well Do You Know Your Fiancé?*"

Luke turned to Amy and grinned. "This should be fun."

Fun? It wasn't the word Amy was thinking of at all.

This was going to be a nightmare.

Luke and Amy sat in two chairs next to each other in the middle of the family room. Her family and friends were so excited that the two of them were engaged. Amy's excitement was nonexistent. She felt like she was sitting in the electric chair waiting for someone to pull the lever.

Luke didn't appear nervous at all.

Maybe he was one of those freaks who embraced uncertainty.

Luke leaned toward Amy and kept his voice low. "I was at an engagement party a few weeks ago, so I know how to get us through this with minimal or no damage."

"Tell me because I'm on the verge of breaking out in hives," Amy whispered.

"Keep your answers ambiguous and we'll be fine."

"Ambiguous . . ."

"Yes. Or even better, go in the opposite direction and exaggerate. Exaggerating will get laughs, which may distract everyone and get you off the hook from having to answer the question."

"That simple, huh?"

"Yup."

"I don't buy it."

"We can do this," Luke said.

Amy shook her head. "We're dead. Dead in the water."

"It'll be fine. Trust me. Do you have any birthmarks?"

She cranked her head in Luke's direction and stared at him. "Pardon me?"

"Birthmarks. It's a common question with this game.

Tell me."

She hesitated. "If I hear a wisecrack out of you, you're a dead man. Got it?"

"Got it."

"Okay . . ." She leaned in closer to Luke. "I have a birthmark on the outside of my right thigh. It's shaped like . . . a gummy bear."

Luke laughed and Amy smacked him on the arm.

"What?" Luke said. "I didn't say a thing."

"Remind me to kill you after I kill Jennie and my dad."

He grinned. "Fine. But for my last meal I would like to have gummy bears."

Another smack to the arm.

"Okay, everyone. Settle down." Dawn approached the middle of the room and stood in front of Amy and Luke. "I have been appointed the hostess with the mostest, so let's get right to it." Dawn shuffled through a stack of three-by-five cards. "On these cards is one question that each of you wrote, so let's begin." She glanced back at Amy and Luke. "Ready?"

"Ready," they both said together.

"Great. Luke, we'll start with you . . . does Amy have any birthmarks? And if so, where?"

Luke turned and gave Amy a knowing smile and winked at her. "She sure does. She's got the cutest birthmark on the outside of her right thigh. It's shaped like a gummy bear."

"Correct! We don't need to confirm that with Amy since we all know that is the truth." Dawn flipped to the next card. "Here's another one for Luke. What is the one thing that makes Amy blush?"

"That's easy," he said turning to her and smiling. "Me. I make her blush."

"Amy, is this true?"

She couldn't admit to that. Then Luke would know he had an effect on her.

That's the last thing she wanted.

"No," Amy said, locking eyes with Luke, but then turning away before she blushed. "That's not true at all."

"Interesting," Dawn said. "Okay, looks like we've already found something Luke didn't know about Amy."

"Or something Amy didn't know about herself," Luke said with confidence.

Dawn laughed. "Good point. Let's do one more question for Luke, and then we'll move on with some questions for Amy." Dawn flipped to the next card in the stack. "Oooh, I like this one. Luke, what is Amy's bra size?"

Laughter filled the room, most likely started from the horrified expression on Amy's face.

What kind of question was that? This is wrong, wrong, wrong.

"I object," Amy said. "Next question."

Dawn wagged a finger at Amy. "Uh-uh. You don't have a say in the matter. Luke? Amy's bra size?"

Luke leaned forward a tad and studied Amy's breasts, scratching his chin and playing up the theatrics.

Amy felt her cheeks heat up.

She crossed her arms, which felt like they made her boobs bigger, so she uncrossed them.

Luke smiled and then leaned back in his chair. "36B."

"Correct!" Dawn said, then pointed to Amy's face. "And it looks like Amy is blushing, so Luke was right on the previous question as well! He does make her blush."

Damn him!

CHAPTER NINE

Luke couldn't remember the last time a woman made him laugh and smile so much. He also couldn't believe he was getting paid to spend the entire week with her. He was having a great time with Amy, and the night and the week were still young. Amy had been paranoid about her family finding out about their fake engagement, but they had nothing to worry about. Except for her father being a little suspicious, everything was going according to plan, and he was confident they could pull it off.

For some reason Amy had her guard up. But why? Was it Luke's age? Maybe his profession? Or maybe he reminded her of someone from her past. But if that was the case why would she have hired him in the first place? No, it was something else.

Luke had no doubts Amy was attracted to him and he sure as hell was attracted to her. Maybe he didn't need to analyze the situation so much since he had already made it crystal clear he didn't have a place for dating in his life. Which meant he didn't have a place for Amy, except for business purposes. He was there because she paid him to do a job, and he was going to damn well do it to the best of his ability. Lucky for him he could have fun at the same time.

"Okay," Dawn said. "It's Amy's turn. Ready?"

"Not even a little," Amy said.

Everyone laughed.

"Perfect," Dawn said, ignoring her. "So . . . what is the sexiest part of Luke's body?"

Luke sat up in his chair.

This should be good.

"Once again, I object to the question," Amy said. "And who asked that, anyway?"

Grams raised her hand. "It may have been me."

"This is a *like* or *dislike*. It has nothing to do with how well I know Luke."

"Are you saying you don't know his body well enough?" Dawn asked. "What a shame. Saving yourself for the wedding night?"

"That's not what I'm saying."

Aunt Barbara held up a finger. "Remind me to give you some massage oil for the honeymoon, Luke. It's a special blend of hinoki, geranium, and coriander. It will knock your socks off."

Luke grinned. "I look forward to being sockless."

Amy jumped in. "Next question."

"Don't be such a stick in the mud," Grams said. "I'd be happy to tell you *my* favorite parts of Luke's body. I have several."

"Are you cheating on me?" Grandpa Leo said.

Grams smiled at Grandpa Leo and patted him on the hand. "Only with my eyes, dear."

"Amy?" Dawn said.

Luke leaned closer to Amy, whispering, "They gave you the easiest question in the world. Pick any body part and you're done with the first question. Don't make our charade any harder than it has to be."

"Fine," Amy whispered.

"We're waiting," Dawn said.

Amy let her eyes roll up and down Luke's body and then crinkled her nose. "He's got a nice butt."

"Amen," Grams yelled out. She turned to Grandpa Leo. "No offense."

"None taken," Grandpa Leo said. "Everyone knows my butt relocated down near the back of my knees during the Jimmy Carter administration."

"I can still reach it with my hand while I'm seated, though." Grams laughed. "I love you no matter where your butt is located."

"I love you, too," Grandpa Leo said, reaching over and kissing Grams on the lips.

Luke glanced over at Amy, grinning. "So . . . you like my butt, huh?"

"You told me to pick a body part, and I did," Amy said. "Randomly. Without any thought going into it."

"Uh-huh. Sure." Luke stood and turned his back to Amy, knowing full well he was playing with fire, but he couldn't help himself because Amy was a kick in the pants. "And you happened to pick my butt as your favorite part."

The slap across his butt cheek was swift and hard.

Cheers came from around the kitchen.

"Yes!" Dawn yelled. "You show him, Amy."

Amy grimaced and opened and closed her fist, glancing down at his butt again. "Is that thing made of steel? How many hours do you spend in the gym every day?"

"I don't go to the gym," Luke said before he could stop himself. Big mistake since everyone was paying attention. She would know he didn't work out with weights since they were getting married. "You *know* that." He winked, hoping she would get a clue.

Amy glanced down at his legs before an *oops, I messed up* look spread across her face. "Of course, I know that. It was a rhetorical question."

Good save.

A loud yell from outside silenced everyone in the kitchen.

Greg got up and flew out the screen door to the backyard.

Luke followed, in case he needed help with whatever was going on.

Grandpa Leo was right behind Luke, looking closer to sixty years old than ninety, the way he was moving.

"Ruben!" Greg yelled, rushing to the man lying on the ground.

It was the ranch hand Amy and Grandpa Leo had mentioned. He was older than Luke had imagined, maybe pushing seventy. His face and hands were dark and weathered, most likely from working in the sun all day. His light blue overalls looked almost gray because of the layer of dirt and dust.

"What happened?" Greg said. "You okay?"

Everyone from inside the house filed to the outside and surrounded Ruben.

Amy stood by Luke's side, a worried look on her face.

Ruben winced, holding his wrist. "Baa Baa got out again. She's on the roof. I tried to get her down but slipped before I could get there. The bale of straw broke my fall. I'll be okay, but I hurt my wrist."

Baa Baa?

Amy must have seen the confused look on Luke's face. "Baa Baa is our goat." She pointed to the roof. "Baa Baa Ganoush. She's been in the family for years and is always a handful. Always getting into things."

Luke helped Ruben to his feet. "Here you go."

"Much obliged," Ruben said. "You must be Luke."

"Yes, sir."

"I'm Ruben. I take care of things around here when I'm not getting old and falling off things."

"A pleasure to meet you, sir." He pointed to Ruben's wrist. "Better get ice on that. And take some ibuprofen while you're at it."

"Good idea."

Aunt Barbara gestured to Ruben's wrist. "I've got oil for that after you're done with the ice. A natural anti-inflammatory with cloves, roses, eucalyptus, and fennel."

Ruben nodded. "Sounds good. I'll take what I can get."

Luke turned and eyed the perimeter of the house, then shot a look back up at the goat on the roof. "How'd she get up there?"

"The hay stack on the side of the house," Ruben said. "I've been meaning to move the bales inside the barn, so it's my own fault."

Luke glanced toward the side of the house and then walked in that direction without saying another word.

"Where are you going?" Amy said.

He stopped and swung around. "To get the goat down."

"Let her be. That's dangerous going up there and you can—"

"Let him do it," Greg said, almost looking like he was daring Luke to go up on the roof. Did Greg want him to fail in front of Amy? It sure seemed like it.

Why didn't he want his daughter to be happy?

Luke wouldn't have been surprised if it had something to do with her ex, Nathan, but that was none of his concern. Right now, the only thing he wanted to do was get the goat down. Not to impress anyone. Not to prove that he could do it. Not to score points with Amy. He wanted to help. Nothing more. Nothing less.

Luke winked at Amy. "I can handle it."

Amy huffed. "You're as stubborn as Baa Baa."

"Well, I don't know her well enough to agree or disagree with you," Luke said, chuckling.

"Baa Baa weighs seventy pounds," Grandpa Leo said. "She's solid as a rock and ornery as hell."

"Good to know," Luke said, wondering why everyone except Greg was trying to stop him. He smiled, thinking of the surprised look on Amy's face. Why would she think it was such a big deal to grab Baa Baa off the roof? Luke had plenty of experience with goats. Had plenty of experience with all farm animals. This wasn't the first time he'd seen a goat on a roof. Wouldn't be the last, either. Maybe while he was up there, he would change Baa Baa's name to something less ridiculous.

"There's the problem," Luke said to himself, eyeing the hay stack on the side of the house. The bales weren't stacked neatly one on top of the other, so they formed perfect steps. Any goat would have seen that as an open invitation to play on the roof.

Luke pulled a handful of hay from one of the bales and stuffed it in his back pocket, then stepped up from one bale to the next until he was on the roof. He worked his way across until he was face-to-face with Baa Baa.

Luke smiled. "You sure are a cute thing. What the heck are you doing up here?"

"Baa."

"Nice to meet you. I'm Luke."

"Baa."

"You have *goat* to be *kid*ding me." He chuckled. "Did you get the joke there?"

"Baa."

"Must be the delivery. I need to work on that."

"What are you two talking about up there?" Amy called out from down below.

"We're bonding. It's what the police do when they're talking someone down off a building."

"Baa Baa is not thinking of suicide. She's a goat."

"Thank you for clarifying."

"I would also like to clarify that I don't want to be a widow before I even get married, so please get back down here."

"Of course, my love," Luke said, impressed that Amy had worked their fake wedding into the discussion. "Be right there."

Luke grabbed the hay from his back pocket and pulled out a single strand from the bunch, sticking it front of Baa Baa's mouth. "Snack time, Baa Baa."

The goat moved forward and snagged it, beginning to chew.

Luke dropped his hand with the rest of the hay down to his side, turned his back on Baa Baa, and headed back to the spot where he'd climbed up.

"She's following you!" Amy said, a surprised tone to her voice.

Luke could feel the pull from Baa Baa nibbling on the hay in his hand, but he held on tight. He got to the edge of the roof, yanked the hay from Baa Baa's mouth, and then jumped down the first two bales, hoping she would follow him.

Baa Baa didn't budge.

He waved his hand. "Come on, now. Don't make me look bad. Put one hoof in front of the other."

"Baa."

"Leave her," Amy said, coming around the side of the house with the rest of the family. "She'll come down eventually."

Amy didn't know he wasn't a quitter.

Luke took two steps back up to the roof. "Plan B. I'll pick her up and bring her down." He stepped back up onto the roof to grab Baa Baa.

"I wouldn't do that," Amy said. "She doesn't like to be picked up."

Luke slid both arms under Baa Baa and lifted her up, holding her against his chest as he climbed back down. He placed Baa Baa back on the ground, handed her the hay again, and wiped his hands on his jeans.

Baa Baa leaned against Luke like a dog would have, finishing the rest of the hay.

"Okay," Amy said. "That was unexpected."

"Another rescue for Luke!" Grandma Betty said. "First

Amy, then the duckling, then Baa Baa. Your fiancé is a regular Superman. Give that man a kiss!"

This job is getting better and better by the minute.

Amy hesitated and then kissed Luke on the cheek.

"What the heck was that?" Jennie asked. "On the lips, please. This isn't *Little House on the Prairie.*"

Luke was sure Amy's niece wanted them to be together. In his mind, that had been a definite *no* when they had met at the Double Deuce, but he had to admit it had gone from a *no* to a *maybe.*

Too bad Amy's body language was saying *no way in hell* in regard to the kiss.

Luke let her off the hook. "We'll have plenty of time for that tonight, if you know what I mean." He winked and pointed to the hay stack. "Speaking of rolling in the hay, those bales need to be moved or she'll go right back up again."

Greg gestured to the John Deere tractor with the hay spear attached and then crossed his arms. "I would invite you to use the tractor, but a city boy like you doesn't know how to—"

"Don't mind if I do." Luke hopped up on the tractor to shut Greg up.

"Luke," Amy said, another worried look on her face.

"Oh, let the man be, Amy," Greg said. "Are you going to question everything he does? That won't make for a happy marriage."

Amy's father cared nothing about her happiness. Greg was daring Luke again. Like he believed he didn't have the mental capacity to operate that machine.

Luke started the tractor and got to work, moving all the bales inside the barn as everyone watched. It didn't take long at all. After he finished, Luke killed the engine and jumped back off.

Greg scowled and looked away.

Ruben came back out from the house, his wrist wrapped in ice. "Thank you for taking care of that."

"Anytime," Luke said. "How does the wrist feel?"

"It's a little swollen, but not too bad."

"Good to hear. Try keeping your wrist above your heart. It'll help minimize swelling by allowing fluid to drain away from the injured area. And don't forget about Aunt Barbara's special oil."

"Already have it, thank you."

Amy stared at Luke again.

"Luke's a doctor, too?" Grandma Betty said.

"Not at all, Grams," Luke chuckled. "Just some things I learned online. You can never be too prepared, you know?" He gestured to Baa Baa. "Where do you keep her?"

Grandpa Leo pointed toward the barn. "We have a covered goat yard over there to the left of the barn."

"I can take a look at where she's getting out. I'll patch it up in a jiffy."

"Not necessary," Greg said. "I already put in a call to Nathan. He'll take care of it in the morning."

"What?" Amy said, taking a step toward her dad. "Why would you do that?"

"Because Nathan knows his way around a farm." Greg glanced at Luke but said nothing else.

Amy's dad was a real piece of work.

"Nice guns," Grandma Betty said, squeezing Luke's arms.

"Grams," Amy said.

"Oh, settle down," Grandma Betty said. "Luke is a

wonderful addition to the family. I think he deserves another kiss!"

"Baa."

"Not you, Baa Baa," Grandma Betty said. "Our dear Amy has the honor."

"Grams—knock it off with the kisses," Amy said. "What about dessert?"

"I second that," Dawn said.

"Okay, okay," Grams said. "Let's all head back inside."

Everyone headed back inside to enjoy warm apple pie with ice cream.

They never did finish that game of *How Well Do You Know Your Fiancé?*, which was a good thing for Luke and Amy. They'd cleared the first hurdle and had great conversation as they enjoyed the dessert.

"Okay," Dawn said, pushing her plate to the side. "Time for gifts."

"What are you talking about now?" Amy asked.

"Engagement parties have gifts. Always." Dawn grabbed a black and white bag that said *Future Mrs.* on the outside and handed it to Amy. "This one is from me."

Amy shook her head. "This was completely unnecessary." She removed the paper from the bag and pulled out a turquoise negligee, unfolding it.

"Hold it up against your body so Luke can have a look," Dawn said.

Amy hesitated but obeyed, holding it up against her body and locking gazes with Luke.

Luke swallowed hard, nodding.

Dawn laughed and pointed to Luke. "That look right there on the man's face tells me I made an excellent choice."

Amy said nothing. She folded up the negligee and placed it back in the bag. Other gifts followed, including champagne and chocolate. Then it was Aunt Barbara's turn.

Aunt Barbara smiled, handing them a box. "I know you said you didn't need any, but you should always have a backup plan in place for getting pregnant. These oils have a special mix of grapefruit, juniper, lavender, and yarrow. She'll be pregnant faster than Luke can put his pants on."

"Aunt Barbara! You know I don't want any kids."

Later that evening, Luke walked side-by-side with Amy to the guesthouse, both in silence. She looked a little apprehensive when she mentioned they should both turn in, and he could only assume it had something to do with the sleeping arrangement. She had nothing to worry about because he had already decided to sleep on the floor.

"So . . ." Amy said, gesturing around the room after they entered the guest house. "This is it."

"I like it," Luke glanced around the room at the fireplace, the oak desk, the TV area, and the king-size bed against the far wall. The place even had a full kitchen. It had a rustic feel to it, mostly earth tones, like a cabin in the mountains. Pictures of horses and dogs and apples covered every open space on the walls. And best of all, there was a couch, so he wouldn't have to sleep on the floor.

Amy pointed toward the open door in between the bed and the window. "That's the bathroom there. I hope you don't like to take baths because we have a walk-in shower."

"That'll do fine."

"Although we have a natural hot springs on the property, if you ever feel like taking a dip."

"Good to know," Luke said.

"Anyway," Amy said, turning to him and crossing her arms. "I've got some rules, so pay close attention."

Luke chuckled and leaned against the desk. "Have you *ever* gone anywhere or done anything without having a rule or a condition?"

She thought about it for a moment. "Can't say that I have."

"Not surprising," Luke said. "Coincidentally, I have a few rules of my own."

"You?" She laughed. "Why should you get to have rules here? This isn't your—"

Luke held up his palm to stop her from talking. "Number one, I get to sleep on the couch. Now, I know you'll try to fight me on this one, but I won't take no for an answer. You're going to have to suffer and take one for the team." He pointed to what had to be the largest bed in the world. "You need to sleep on that big, fluffy, comfortable, supportive bed that sleeps ten."

Amy broke eye contact and looked away, her bottom lip quivering.

Luke cocked his head to the side, trying to see her face. "Do I see the beginning of what might appear to be laughter?"

"No," Amy said, still avoiding eye contact.

"Could have fooled me . . . Rule number two, no prancing around here in that nightie they gave you. Sleep in layers if possible. Multiple layers. I'd be happy to duct tape a sleeping bag around your body."

"It's summer. I'm not going to sleep in layers."

"You're a beautiful woman and it would be impossible not to look at you if you're wearing something skimpy."

Amy hesitated. "I'm forty-five years old."

"So?"

"You're thirty-five."

"And?"

Amy sighed. "Nothing. I'm going to brush my teeth and get ready for bed. I'll empty my suitcase in the morning."

"Same here. I'll take a shower when you're all done in there, if you don't mind."

Amy glanced at his chest. "Okay . . ." She pulled a few things from her suitcase and entered the bathroom, closing the door behind her.

Luke sat on the couch and checked the email on his phone as he waited for Amy to take care of her nightly business in the bathroom. When she came out she was wearing a *Seinfeld* t-shirt that said "No soup for you!" It hung down to mid-thigh. She slipped into the bed.

Damn.

Luke had never been a big fan of *Seinfeld*. Had never been a big fan of soup, either.

Until now.

He guessed it didn't matter what Amy wore. She would still cause the same reaction in him.

Luke grabbed some things from his suitcase, summoned all the willpower he had not to glance over at Amy in the bed, and then headed to the shower.

Fifteen minutes later, he dried himself off, slipped into his silk boxers and walked out of the bathroom toward the couch, figuring Amy would already be asleep.

Not even close.

"What are you doing?" Amy said, covering her eyes like she was trying to shield herself from the blinding sun.

Luke stopped in his tracks and turned to her. "What do you mean?"

"I mean, why are you dressed like *that*?" She waved a hand at his body as she peeked between a few fingers of the other hand.

Luke stared down at his body. "Dressed like I'm ready to go to bed? That's because I'm ready to go to bed." He glanced down at his boxers again. "We're both adults here, right?"

"Yes," she said. "And *that* is the problem."

"I don't see a problem at all," Luke said. "If we were at the beach I would wear trunks. What's the difference?"

She glanced down at his boxers again and then shot her gaze back up to meet his. "We're not at the beach, that's the difference."

"What are you, the forty-five-year-old virgin?"

She sighed. "Not funny. Look—it's getting late and I would like to read a little before turning off the light." She grabbed her Kindle and flipped it open.

"Of course," Luke said, unfolding the thin blanket sitting on the end of the couch. He stretched out on the couch and covered himself with the blanket, pulling it up to the middle of his stomach. It wasn't cold, so he didn't need much at all.

Why was Amy acting so weird? She was a grown woman. He turned to his side and glanced over at her on the bed, the Kindle covering her face.

As if she could see through the Kindle, she lowered it and blew out a desperate breath. "What?"

Luke shrugged. "Nothing. Just curious what you were reading."

She stared at him, not answering.

"Fine," Luke said. "You don't have to tell me. Can I say one more thing and that will be it?"

More staring.

"I'm enjoying this."

"Enjoying what?" Amy said. "Torturing me?"

"How am I torturing you?"

"By being . . . you!"

He nodded. "And what am I?"

"You're . . . nice!"

Luke nodded again. "Ahhhh. The dreaded *nice*. The kiss of death with the ladies, I know." He thought about it for a beat. "I could try to be mean if that floats your boat. How's this?" He grabbed the orange pillow from the couch and spiked it on the floor.

She glanced at the pillow on the floor.

Luke could have sworn she was on the verge of cracking a smile.

The smile never came.

Luke chuckled. "Right . . ." He picked up the pillow, dusted it off, and placed it back on the couch. "Well, I guess I'm stuck with nice then. And there are far worse things to be. Anyway, I'm enjoying your company, and being here, and helping you. I wish I understood why you're so uptight."

"I'm not uptight."

"The only thing I can think of is that Jennie was right on the money with her diagnosis. Anyway, good night."

There was no way Amy would let Luke have the last word.

"What diagnosis?" Amy said.

He stifled a laugh and glanced back over in her direction. "You know . . . the one about you being a little *loco* because you never kiss with tongue. Now, I'm not a doctor, but I'm sure I have a cure for that insanity."

A bed pillow flew across the room and smacked Luke in the face.

He couldn't hold back the laughter this time. "What was that for?"

"You know what that was for. There will be no more kissing between us. Got it? And if you want to sleep with Baa Baa tonight, keep talking."

He chuckled again and fluffed up the pillow. "Thanks for the extra pillow."

Amy didn't answer, lifting the Kindle back up in front of her face.

Luke wondered how long she would keep up the act. They had some serious chemistry going on between them, but she was playing it off like it didn't exist. And she could talk all she wanted about there not being anymore kisses between them until she was blue in the face and raw in the throat, but there was one thing he knew for sure.

Another kiss was coming.

CHAPTER TEN

The next morning, Amy shot up to a seated position in bed, startled from the loud knock on the guesthouse door. She rubbed her eyes and looked over at the alarm clock.

"Wonderful," she mumbled to herself, seeing it was ten minutes after the butt-crack of dawn. She glanced over at Luke who was snoring up a storm, oblivious to the knock. The blanket he'd been using had fallen to the floor during the night, revealing his body.

"Luke?" Grandpa Leo called from outside after another knock.

"Pssssst," Amy whispered in Luke's direction.

Too bad he didn't move a muscle.

"Luke," she tried again.

Nothing.

Another knock on the door. "Luke? You in there? Amy?"

"Maybe they went for a walk," Grams said from outside. "Check the door."

The handle jiggled.

"Nope," Grandpa Leo said. "Locked."

Amy grabbed a pillow and flung it at Luke, connecting with his face.

"Huh? What?" Luke said, setting the pillow off to the side. He sat up and looked in Amy's direction, grinning. "Good morning, sugar. Is this how you wake up your men?"

"Shhhhh," Amy said. "I don't have *men*. And keep it down. Grandpa Leo and Grams are outside."

"And?"

"You're on the couch and I'm in the bed. We're supposed to be sleeping together."

"Mighty forward of you."

Amy hurled a second pillow in Luke's direction, but this time he caught it and flung it right back.

"A pillow fight as foreplay . . ." he said. "That's a first."

Another knock at the door.

"What's the big deal?" Luke asked, looking over at the door. "Isn't it locked?"

"Yes, but they have a key."

"They would just come in?"

"In a heartbeat."

"You've got a key," Grams said. "Use it."

"What did I tell you?" Amy could hear keys jingling outside and waved Luke over to the bed like it was a matter of life and death. "Please."

"As you wish," Luke said, popping up from the couch and sliding into the bed next to Amy, scooting closer. "You smell great."

"Keep your hands to yourself."

Luke sighed. "Here come the rules again."

"Obey them."

"We should spoon," Luke said, ignoring her. "You know, to make it look more realistic."

"Fine. Spoon."

The door flew open.

"Oh!" Grandpa Leo said. "Sorry about that. Didn't think you were here."

"Good morning," Luke said, scooting even closer to Amy so their legs and arms were touching. "Just cuddling with my wife-to-be." He reached his arm under her neck, cupped her shoulder and pulled her halfway onto his chest.

Amy's heart rate headed north.

She couldn't think straight.

So she did the first thing that came to her mind.

"Ouch!" Luke said after Amy pinched him on the leg.

Grams smiled. "You crazy kids. Breakfast is at seven thirty."

Amy glanced over at the clock again and then arched an eyebrow. "It's six in the morning. I know you didn't come here to give us a ninety-minute warning about breakfast. What's going on?"

"I take credit for our granddaughter's brains," Grams said. "Anyway, your grandpa has a brilliant idea."

"And this couldn't have waited until breakfast?" Amy asked.

"It would be too late by then."

Grandpa Leo took a step toward Luke's side of the bed. "We really could use your help."

"Of course," Luke said. "Whatever you need."

"We appreciate that," Grandpa Leo said. "Nathan is

coming over at eight to repair the fence where Baa Baa keeps getting through. If we want to beat Amy's dad at the game he's playing, we need to stay one step ahead of him and Nathan. I thought you could repair the fence before Nathan shows up. We normally have Ruben do it, but his wrist doesn't look good, even with Barbara's oils. He can get you anything you need. I don't think it will take more than an hour to fix and then we can send Nathan on his merry little way when he shows up."

"Count me in," Luke said.

"That won't work," Amy said. "Dad will find something else for Nathan to do."

"Then I'll do that, too."

Amy shook her head. "You don't get it. My dad won't stop. He's obsessed with me and Nathan being together. He thinks if we're together I'll move back to Julian. He'll keep coming up with things for Nathan to do and he won't give up."

"Neither will I. I told you I'm not a quitter." Luke looked back to Grandpa Leo. "Give me five minutes and I'll be ready."

"Great," Grams said, leaving with Grandpa Leo and closing the door behind them.

"This is a bad idea," Amy said. "You don't have to do this."

"Do what?" Luke said, glancing down at her Seinfeld t-shirt. "Cuddle?"

Amy pulled the covers up higher. "You're not taking this seriously."

"I always take cuddling seriously."

Amy pushed Luke away and pointed to the floor. "You can get out of the bed now."

He nodded. "I need a moment, if you don't mind."

"Why?"

"Well . . . you know. For certain parts to settle down."

Amy glanced down toward his torso.

She had felt something, but thought he was jabbing her with his knee, not his—

"I told you . . . I find you very attractive."

Amy popped out of bed. "Quit trying to change the subject. I didn't hire you to do physical labor. I hired you to be my fiancé."

Sure, he'd gotten Baa Baa down off the roof and could rearrange the hay with the tractor, but working the farm was hard work and something an actor would have no experience with. The last thing she wanted was for him to get hurt.

Luke caught Amy staring at his biceps.

Wonderful.

He winked at her and said, "Muscles are meant to be used. Anyway, I don't mind at all. That's what family's for, right?"

Even though they weren't his family, there was no use trying to stop him.

Luke was as stubborn as Baa Baa.

Five minutes later he was out the door and Amy's mind wandered back to the half-naked man in her bed and his three little words that had gotten her blood pumping.

We should spoon.

She'd be lying if she said she wasn't happy he had suggested it.

She'd be lying if she said her body didn't react in a certain tingly way when he'd held her.

She'd be lying if she said she didn't want more.

Luke headed over to the goat area, a big smile on his face. It was a beautiful morning, the birds were singing, the roosters were crowing, and a feisty woman was back in the guesthouse pretending she wasn't attracted to him. Luke had caught her checking out his arms and chest. And even when he scooted closer to her in bed when her grandparents showed up, she didn't resist or move away. He could have sworn there was even one moment where she relaxed into him. Although it could have been his imagination, he doubted it was.

Enough of that fantasy.

Luke had work to do, which he was looking forward to. He'd never been afraid of some physical labor and he had been honest with Amy when he had said the muscles were meant to be used. Nobody had ever called Luke a slacker and nobody ever would.

Grandpa Leo and Ruben waved Luke over as he approached the goat pen.

"Mornin'," Ruben said.

"Mornin'," Luke said. "How's the wrist feeling?"

"You'd still be sleeping this morning if it was a little better. It's tender."

"Sorry to hear that."

"I'm the one who's sorry. I feel bad putting you to work when you're here to celebrate your upcoming wedding. I usually have extra help around here, but a worker quit on me this week, so we're short-handed."

Luke waved him off. "It's no big deal. I enjoy this kind of stuff. Anyway, this will help with Amy and her situation with the ex. I'm all for it."

Grandpa Leo slapped Luke on the back. "You're a good

man. You're also Amy's ticket to freedom and my ticket to peace since I'm always bickering back and forth with Greg about Nathan. That man isn't good enough for my grand-daughter and I look forward to the day I never see him again. Even if it puts a thorn in my son's side."

Luke rubbed his hands together. "Let's get started then."

The three entered the goat area and Grandpa Leo closed the gate behind them.

Luke surveyed the area. "All this for one goat, huh?"

Grandpa Leo chuckled. "I guess Baa Baa's a little spoiled." He pointed to the fence in the corner. "There's the problem area right over there."

Luke nodded. "Ahhhh."

The fence was way too low, Luke could see that right away. Even a three-legged goat with bad hips could jump over it since it was less than four feet high. It was an easy fix.

"Do you have any of that goat wire lying around?" Luke asked.

Ruben pointed to the yard next to the barn where the tractor was parked. "Over there. We've got steel, wood, wire, posts, you name it. Tools are in the barn."

"Perfect," Luke said.

Luke got to work, and an hour later the fence was fixed. There was no way Baa Baa would get out again unless they wanted him to be out or someone left the gate open.

"Looks great," Ruben said, testing the sturdiness of the new section of wire by shaking it with his good arm. "I should've done that last year. Guess I'm slowing down in my old age."

"Don't go beating yourself up about it," Grandpa Leo said. "You get enough of that from Greg." He turned to Luke.

"Amy's dad is a ball-buster around here. Ruben is still a competent and strong worker." He chuckled. "When he's not falling off roofs, that is."

Ruben shook his head, "My body is in its seventies, but my mind still says I'm twenty-five."

The three shared a laugh together.

"What's so funny?" Greg asked, approaching the goat pen with another man who Luke assumed had to be Nathan. "What the—" He stopped when he spotted the repaired fence, his eyes shooting back to Luke and then down to the wire cutters in his hand. "What do you think you're doing? I told you Nathan would fix that."

Grandpa Leo stepped forward. "Why does it matter who fixes it? It needed to be fixed and Luke offered. Did a damn fine job, too."

Nathan eyed Luke from head to toe and shifted his weight from one leg to the other. "This is Amy's fiancé?"

Greg nodded. "For now."

Unbelievable.

Amy's dad had a serious chip on his shoulder, but Luke wasn't going to take crap from him or anybody else.

"Greg's right," Luke said. "I'm Amy's fiancé *for now*, because soon we'll be married. I can't be a fiancé forever, can I?" He took a step toward Nathan and extended his hand. "Luke Jenkins."

He was there to get rid of Nathan, but that didn't mean he needed to be a jerk about it. The guy would get the hint sooner or later. Hopefully sooner.

Nathan accepted Luke's hand, gripping it hard. "Nathan Pillsbury . . . like the biscuits, but not related."

Luke stifled a laugh as the Dough Boy tried to squeeze

his hand harder, as Greg had done the day before. Luke returned the squeeze and could see Nathan's eyes open wider with surprise. Nathan ground his teeth and continued to squeeze.

Who was this joker?

First impressions were pretty accurate, and Nathan appeared to be a giant weasel. That made Luke wonder what Amy had seen in him or what her dad saw in him. He would give the man the benefit of the doubt since there was sometimes more than meets the eye.

Sometimes.

Luke knew nothing about them or how long they had been together. Amy was done with the man and Nathan must have assumed that if he squeezed Luke's hand hard enough fresh orange juice would come out.

Luke glanced down at his hand locked with Nathan's. "You almost done?"

Nathan pulled his hand away, opening and closing it a few times. He was lucky Luke hadn't applied much pressure or the man would have ended up with a fracture.

"Anyone can fix a fence," Greg said. "Come on, Nathan. There are plenty more important things for you to do around here."

Nathan and Greg turned to walk away.

"I'd be happy to help," Luke asked. "The day is young."

Greg stopped and turned back around, giving Luke a *don't mess with me* look. "No offense, but I'm sure the things we need to get done around here are beyond the scope of work for someone who likes to sport aprons and baste chicken breasts with teriyaki sauce."

What a dick.

"I'm *man enough* to admit if there's something I can't do, but I'm always willing to—"

Greg held up the palm of his hand to stop Luke from speaking. "No need. Like I said—I've got a competent man right here to handle the job. Ready, Nathan?"

"Ready," Nathan said, stepping in front of Luke to head toward the gate.

"Oh, let the man help, for goodness sake," Grandpa Leo said, shaking his head in disgust. "I don't understand how you came from my seed. There had to be a mix-up at the hospital when we brought you home."

Nathan stopped, waiting for Luke's reaction.

Greg hesitated and then glared at Luke. "Why do you want to help so bad? What's in it for you?"

"Nothing but the satisfaction of knowing I helped," Luke said. "We're family now and it would be a pleasure."

Something flashed in Greg's eyes. Surprise, with the slightest hint of understanding.

Too bad it was gone in an instant.

"Fine," Greg said. "About three hundred of the apple trees on the north side of the orchard are not getting sufficient water. Could be an all day job to locate the problem and repair it, but we need it done today."

It was obvious Amy's dad was testing Luke to see if he would back down from his offer of helping since it could take him all day to fix. Not a chance.

"Piece of cake," Luke said, winking at Greg and then slapping Nathan on the back. "I've got this." He moved toward the gate, wondering if this would shut them both up after he fixed the problem.

Most likely not if what Amy had said was any indication.

My dad won't stop. He'll keep coming up with things for Nathan to do.

Even if that was the case it didn't matter.

Luke enjoyed a challenge.

And he was enjoying Amy's company.

That was all the motivation he needed.

CHAPTER ELEVEN

"Good morning." Amy entered the kitchen for breakfast and walked straight to the coffeepot to pour herself a cup. She glanced over at the platters of food on the kitchen island, all prepared by Grams and all waiting to be served and eaten. Pancakes, cheesy scrambled eggs, and bacon. It smelled like heaven.

"There's my sweetie pie," Grandpa Leo said, sitting down at the table with a full plate of food. "Get your grub on while it's hot. Grams went to go pick a few lemons from the tree. She made everything with extra love today since you're here."

"She always makes it with extra love," Amy said, smiling and adding cream and sugar to her coffee. "One of these days she'll quit. She doesn't need to do all this."

Grandpa Leo chuckled. "Don't count on it. She's a giver. Always has been. Plus, it keeps her young."

Amy gave her coffee a few stirs, took her first sip, and sighed with pleasure before kissing Grandpa Leo on the cheek. "You married well."

"You got *that* right."

Grams was eighty-five years old and still loved cooking for the family, except when she was in the mood for pizza like last night. She'd been told by the family more than a few times she didn't need to make any meals ever again, but she never listened. She said it brought her great joy to see the smiles on everyone's faces as they ate. She also believed, as Luke did, that muscles were meant to be used.

Speaking of Luke, he hadn't returned to the guest house after leaving this morning to fix Baa Baa's fence. Amy assumed he would be seated at the kitchen table with a big appetite and an even bigger plate of food after the morning work.

"Where's Luke?" Amy asked.

"He's working on the irrigation system in the north orchard, thanks to your father." Grandpa Leo shook his head. "Poor guy. Most people don't know squat about irrigation. I wouldn't be surprised if he's out there all day."

Amy set her coffee on the table next to Grandpa Leo. "Please tell me you're joking."

"Wish I was," he said, spreading butter across his stack of pancakes and then drenching it with syrup. "I think we descended from baboons. Maybe I should've asked for one of those ancestry test thing-a-ma-bobs for my birthday. Your dad is—"

"Hungry," Greg said, entering the kitchen and grabbing a plate. "I thought it would be best to finish your sentence before I heard something I didn't like."

Amy was ready to tell her dad off, but Nathan walked in right behind him. She opened and closed her mouth, not knowing what to say.

Nathan was in his usual attire: jeans, white t-shirt, and

boots. He was even more tanned than last year and his blond hair seemed to be a little thinner on top. She preferred Luke's hair and had the urge to run her fingers through it.

Why am I thinking about that?

Amy wasn't interested in Luke.

Then why was she comparing him to Nathan?

And why was her mind back on Luke and his silk boxers?

"There's that smile I love," Nathan said, locking eyes with Amy and pointing to her face.

Great.

Nathan thought her smile was for him and it most certainly was not. In fact, she had no idea she had been smiling.

"How long has it been?" Nathan asked.

He knew exactly how long it had been.

"A year—that's how long." Greg forked a stack of pancakes onto his plate and took a seat across from Amy. "I guess she doesn't appreciate her family or her hometown enough to come back any more than that."

"I only get a week off every year and I always come here," Amy said, trying to prevent herself from getting worked up.

"You've got weekends," Greg said.

She didn't, since most weddings happened on Saturdays and Sundays, but she would waste her breath telling her dad that again since they'd had this same conversation more than a few times. And it always ended up with the same result. He would have a satisfied look on his face for making Amy feel like crap, and she would storm off to another room.

"Take a seat, Nathan," Greg said. "Next to Amy."

"I'm saving this seat for Luke," Amy said, patting the wooden chair.

Greg smirked. "You may be waiting a while."

"Good morning," Jennie said, also entering the kitchen and going straight for the bacon. She plucked a piece from the platter and took a bite. "Mmm, mmm, mmm." She got a plate from the counter and piled it high with bacon.

Amy stared at Jennie's plate. "You're only going to eat bacon?"

Jennie picked up a bacon strip and let it hover in front of her mouth. "This is the first course. Grams makes the best bacon. Where is she?"

"Right here," Grams said, coming in from the backyard with a basket of lemons. She placed them on the counter. "It's a beautiful day. I saw Luke and he said he'd be here in a couple of minutes after he cleaned off his boots. I told him he didn't need to do that, but he kept insisting." She glanced over at Amy. "Such a nice man. Stubborn, but nice. He also said the irrigation system is not what he expected."

"Of course not," Greg said, a smug, satisfied look on his face. "I knew he wouldn't be able to handle the job." He turned to Nathan and winked. "You can take care of it after breakfast and show him how it's done."

"It would be a pleasure, sir," Nathan said.

"If you knew he wouldn't be able to handle the job why did you let him go out there and try to do it?" Amy asked, on the verge of exploding.

He didn't answer.

"You have nothing to say?" Amy asked. "Does it give you pleasure to watch people fail?"

Greg set his fork down. "Hey, it's not my fault he doesn't know what he's doing."

"Luke isn't an irrigation expert. He wanted to help. And

even if he was an expert, we didn't come here to work. We came to celebrate Grandpa Leo's birthday and celebrate the harvest. Celebrations mean good times. *Happy* times. Well, I don't feel happy right now. And I won't stand for it when you say something against Luke. That's my fiancé you're talking about."

Luke entered the kitchen and kissed Amy on the cheek. "Fiancé has such a nice ring to it, don't you think?"

"Grab a plate, Loverboy," Grams said, pointing to the kitchen island. "Help yourself to whatever you fancy."

"Mighty kind of you," Luke said, getting a plate. "Don't mind if I do."

Amy had been putting up with her dad's bullshit behavior for way too long. It all started when her mom died. She'd let him get away with his rudeness because he was going through a lot. But what about her? She had lost her mom! That didn't give him the right to disrespect people. Enough was enough. She had to speak up, but not now. The last thing she wanted was a family feud right before Grandpa Leo's birthday. She would say something before she headed home, for sure.

Greg cleared his throat. "I told you it was a complex irrigation system. Don't feel bad you couldn't repair it."

"Who said I didn't repair it?" Luke said, focused on the cheesy eggs and not even making eye contact with Greg. He scooped two helpings of the eggs onto his plate and then added a couple of strips of bacon and three pancakes. Luke winked at Amy and then slid into the chair next to her, kissing her on the cheek again. "Did you miss me?"

"Oodles," Amy said, loving how relaxed Luke was and how her dad hadn't affected him one bit. Had he fixed the irrigation system or had he said that to shut him up? It didn't matter. The shocked look on her dad's face was priceless and she could have kissed Luke for that.

"Would you like coffee, Luke?" Grams said.

Luke nodded. "Would love some. Thank you."

"Cream and sugar?"

"Yes, ma'am. If you don't mind."

"I don't mind at all. That's why we've got it."

The table was silent as Greg tapped his fingers on the table.

Grams poured a cup of coffee for Luke, added cream and sugar, and stirred it before setting it down on the table in front of him. "Here you go."

"Thanks, Grams."

"Anytime, sweetie."

"Excuse me," Greg said, a frustrated look on his face. "Are you done? I'm trying to chat with Luke about the irrigation."

Luke poured syrup on top of his pancakes and set the bottle down. "Sorry, sir. Go for it. What would you like to know?" He took a bite of the pancakes.

"You seem to be hinting that you repaired the irrigation."

"Hinting?" Luke said, finally looking across the table to make eye contact with Amy's dad. "I didn't mean to hint." He smiled at Grams. "These are the best pancakes ever. Thank you kindly."

Grams placed a hand on her chest. "It was my pleasure, dear."

Greg stared at Luke, his nostrils flaring. "Did you or did you not repair the irrigation?"

Luke finished chewing and wiped his mouth with the napkin. "Yes. I did. I told you—piece of cake."

"That's what I'm talkin' about," Grandpa Leo said. "He's the jack of all trades."

"That's impossible," Greg said. "You weren't even out there an hour."

"Was it that long?" Luke asked, glancing up at the clock on the kitchen wall and frowning. "I must be getting slow in my old age."

"You and me both," Grandpa Leo said. "What was it? A leak?"

Luke took a sip of his coffee and set the cup back down, shaking his head. "Not a leak. It looked like someone changed the water application rate in the north orchard. It didn't match up with the others."

Grandpa Leo pointed across the table at Luke. "That would be my son."

Greg hesitated. "It was Ruben who changed it."

"But *you* were the one who told him to lower it."

"We were trying to improve soil infiltration and reduce runoff and erosion," Greg said.

Luke nodded. "Not a bad idea, but it gets tricky because you need to consider the evaporative losses, which may increase in the summer months. Then there's the potential of wind distortion increase and moisture stress."

Greg opened his mouth and closed it.

Amy patted Luke's hand. "That's my fiancé."

Okay, he was a fake fiancé, but still she felt closer to him, knowing he put her dad in his place. Amy was shocked by Luke's knowledge, but in a good way. Who was Luke Jenkins and how did an actor know so much about farm irrigation? And mechanical bull riding, for that matter? He wasn't a cowboy, so it made little sense.

He was, however, a wonderful man.

Knock it off.

"You need rotators that will provide a hundred and ten percent overlap," Luke added. "Any less and you run the risk of water deprivation. Plus, the overlap will improve the root development and the general vigor of the trees."

"Go figure," Amy said, impressed even more by what Luke said. "All these years in the apple business and I had no idea trees had vigor."

"Like your fiancé," Jennie said, who had been so quietly devouring her leaning tower of bacon that Amy forgot she was even at the table. "Isn't it time for another kiss?"

"Knock it off," Amy said, even though the thought of another kiss with Luke was tempting.

So tempting.

She must have lost her mind because at that moment she was considering leaning over and planting a kiss on Luke's lips. That would shock the hell out of him, she was sure about that. It would shock the hell out of her dad, too.

Maybe she should . . .

Amy glanced at Luke's lips and—

Ruben rushed into the kitchen out of breath, his wrist still wrapped in an elastic bandage. "Dip Shit is on the property again."

Dip Shit was the young bull from the Johnson property next door. He got into as much trouble as Baa Baa. In fact, just a few weeks ago Dip Shit had gotten onto their property and ran into the water well, causing a lot of damage. The family had insurance to cover such accidents, but it was the downtime for repairs that slowed down the operation and knocked everything off schedule. Apple farming was almost an exact science and just the slightest setback could be devastating for the business.

"Son of a . . ." Greg said. "Where is he this time?"

"By the well again, but I can't do a thing with this wrist. I need help."

"What is it with that bull?" Greg said, standing and shaking his head. "We need to get him out of there now. Let's go, Nathan."

Luke jumped to his feet before Nathan, his breakfast still untouched. "I can take care of it. Is he aggressive?"

"Nah. He's pretty mellow," Grandpa Leo said. "As long as you don't piss him off."

"Good. I need a horse and a lasso."

Greg waved Luke off. "Nice try, but this isn't the Wild, Wild West. Dip Shit is already a thousand pounds and growing every day. Nathan, you can use your truck."

"You bet," Nathan said. "You always come up with the best ideas, sir."

"Push him out toward the south gate and the Johnsons can deal with him after that. Someone get Will Johnson on the phone and tell him I will stop buying his meat if he keeps this up. Ready, Nathan?"

"Yes, sir. Anything for you and Amy."

"What do I have to do with it?" Amy asked.

Nathan winked and followed Greg out the door.

"That looks like a disaster waiting to happen," Grandpa Leo said. "Get Stardust out for Luke. She's got brains *and* beauty."

Luke grinned. "Like Amy, then."

"Exactly!"

Amy flushed, but preferred to stay on topic. "You sure about this?"

"About us?" Luke said.

"About lassoing a bull. You could get hurt."

He grinned. "Piece of cake. Let's go."

Amy led Luke to the barn where she grabbed a lasso and some gloves for him. A minute later they were standing in front of Stardust's stall.

"She's a beauty," Luke said, reaching across the stall door to pet her.

Amy nodded. "Don't tell the other horses, but she's my favorite."

After Luke saddled up Stardust, Ruben pointed him in the direction of the water well. Amy followed right behind in the ranch ATV, stopping alongside Luke when they got there to watch Nathan in action.

"What a joke," Luke said, watching Nathan drive up one of the rows of trees right by Dip Shit. "Does he think he'll catch him that way?"

"*He* thinks so, but it's not going to happen," Amy said.

"Take the next row!" Greg yelled, trying to guide Nathan but doing a terrible job.

Nathan stuck his truck in reverse, backed up about twenty feet, and then shifted back to drive, going around the well in pursuit of Dip Shit. Amy wanted to tell him it was useless since the bull could easily hide behind one of the apple trees, but her dad would tell her to let them do their jobs. Dip Shit ran behind an apple tree and down the next row of trees just as Amy thought he would.

Greg waved his arms frantically. "What the hell are you doing? Go past Dip Shit on the next row and flip a U-turn so you're facing him. Then push him toward the south gate."

Nathan followed Greg's instructions and punched it down the next row, flying past the bull. Then he slammed on the brakes and cranked the steering wheel so the truck slid around to face Dip Shit.

Dip Shit eyed Nathan's truck, probably wondering what the heck the idiot was doing.

Nathan revved his engine.

Dip Shit huffed.

Nathan revved again.

Dip Shit huffed again.

He looked pissed off.

Not good.

"He's going to play chicken with a bull?" Luke said.

"It appears so," Amy said.

Nathan revved his engine one more time.

"Well, I'll be . . ." Luke said. "It looks like Dip Shit is going to—"

Dip Shit charged at Nathan's new truck.

Bulls didn't typically charge vehicles, so it was a sight to see. Dip Shit was acting more like a mama cow protecting her calf than a bull.

"This isn't going to be pretty," Luke said. "I've got my money on Dip Shit."

"That's a good bet," Amy said.

Dip Shit head-butted Nathan's truck with a loud boom, shattering the headlight on the right side. The bull stepped back, the bumper of the truck attached to his horns. He shook his head and the bumper fell to the dirt with a loud thud.

"No!" Nathan yelled, hanging out the window and trying to survey the damage.

Better his truck than the water well or one of the trees.

Dip Shit strolled past an apple tree as if nothing ever

happened, stopping to graze near the fence between the two properties.

"I guess that's my cue," Luke said. "This shouldn't take long." He snapped the reins and Stardust took off, leaving a trail of dust in the air and surprise in Amy's head.

Shouldn't take long? How could he have so much confidence?

Luke flew past Nathan's truck on Stardust, looking like a natural on the horse.

Was there anything he couldn't do?

Luke raised his arm up, swung the lasso around four times and then let it fly, the lasso wrapping around Dip Shit's head and horns on the first attempt. Luke pulled on the lasso, tightening it around Dip Shit. Surprisingly, the bull didn't care, continuing to graze on the tall grass.

Amy shook her head in disbelief, having never seen someone lasso a bull before. And Luke was right, taking less than a minute to catch Dip Shit. He slowly led the bull toward the south gate where Will Johnson was waiting to take him back to his property.

Amy sat there watching from the ATV, speechless. If her mind had been a member of a frequent flyer program, she would have had free trips racked up for life because just then it was traveling a thousand miles a second.

Something didn't add up. What was going on here? None of it made sense. Luke knew a lot about farms and tractors and animals. He knew so much about everything.

Too much.

The only way he could have that much knowledge about being a cowboy was if he—

"No," she mumbled to herself in horror.

Amy was sure now she had made a horrible mistake.

That was the only logical explanation.

All along she thought she'd hired an actor to play the part of her fake cowboy fiancé, but now she was certain he wasn't acting at all.

Luke was *a real* cowboy.

An honest-to-goodness, handsome, kind, funny, good-hearted cowboy.

Amy let that sink in a little longer before shaking her head in disbelief.

"Oh, boy," she said to herself. "My heart is going to be in serious trouble."

CHAPTER TWELVE

Luke put Stardust back into her stall and began to brush her as Amy watched in silence. He enjoyed riding her, and he hoped he'd have a chance to do it again this week. Grandpa Leo was right. The horse was something special. Beauty and brains. Just like Amy, although Luke wondered why his fake fiancée was suddenly so quiet. Her silence didn't make much sense at all. She thanked him after he got Dip Shit off the property, but those were the only two words that came out of her mouth. Well, there was one other thing. A question.

Who are you?

It had caught him off guard.

He'd tried to answer the question, but then she'd cut him off.

"Never mind," she had said. "It doesn't matter now."

Luke was sure she was mad at him, but why? Since they'd arrived he'd been as helpful as possible. He made sure everyone believed without a doubt they were a real couple about to get married.

After a few more strokes, Luke hung the brush up and pulled a carrot from a stash Amy had pointed out earlier.

He gave the carrot to Stardust and smiled. "Here you go, girl."

Stardust leaned forward and grabbed the carrot, chewing away.

"You ever met a horse who didn't like carrots?" Luke asked, trying to break the ice and get Amy to say something. "I know I haven't."

"Why didn't you tell me you were a cowboy?" Amy asked.

He glanced over at Amy, pulling another carrot from the bag. "I don't understand the question."

"Playing dumb. That's good."

Luke scratched the side of his face. "Okay. I'll try to play smart and figure this out on my own since I left my female decoder at home. You want to know *why* I didn't tell you I was a cowboy, and I will answer by asking *you* . . . wasn't it obvious?"

"No."

Luke chuckled. "Okay, then. Let me see if I've got this right . . . You met me in a cowboy bar. I look like a cowboy. I dress like a cowboy. *And* I act like a cowboy." He squished his eyebrows together, confused. "Maybe I should ask you how you couldn't know I was a cowboy."

Amy huffed. "Right. Like this is all my fault."

"What fault? I thought you hired me because I was a cowboy."

"Wrong," Amy said, grabbing the bag of carrots and pulling another one out for Stardust. "I hired you because I thought you were an actor who was going to *play the part* of a cowboy."

"Did you eat some poisonous mushrooms?"

Amy crossed her arms. "Not funny."

"Why would you want an actor when you could have the real thing?"

She opened her mouth and closed it.

Luke chuckled, even more confused than before. "And why would you think I was an actor in the first place?"

"Many reasons," Amy said, sighing. "What about the show at the Hillcrest Theater? How do you explain that?"

"If *show* is another word for *business meeting*, then you're right."

Amy didn't respond.

"I don't get it," Luke said. "Things are going great, right? Everyone believes we're together."

"Yes, but this new revelation complicates things."

"*What* revelation?"

"Never mind."

Luke was thinking those were her two favorite words.

"Are you going to tell me what's going on here?" he asked.

"Forget about it," Amy said, pointing to the main house. "Let's get you some food. You must be starving."

That was a good sign. Amy couldn't have been that pissed off at him or she would have let him starve to death. And she was right. He was hungry.

Luke rubbed Stardust on the side of the face. "See you later, girl." He walked alongside Amy back to the house, but then stopped. "I'm having a revelation of my own."

"Congratulations," Amy said, continuing to walk.

"You're attracted to me and you don't want to be. That's what this is all about. Admit it."

He preferred to call it like he saw it. Why should they beat around the bush?

Amy stopped, took a few steps back toward Luke, and placed her hands on her hips. "I will not admit such a thing."

"Then you are."

"I didn't say that."

"You didn't *not* say that."

Amy smirked. "That's a double negative."

"Which turns into a positive which means you *are* attracted to me."

"That's ridiculous."

"Not really," Luke said. "You said you wouldn't admit to it, but you also didn't deny it, which is admitting it."

"If that makes your ego happier then we can go with that."

"I prefer to go somewhere else. Out."

Amy jerked her head back. "Out? Where?"

"On a date."

"That is the sweetest thing," Grams said, coming from the orchard with a basket of apples. "This is one romantic man, still thinking of dating you when you're about to get married. That's how you keep the romance alive. This man's a keeper."

"Thanks, Grams." Luke reached for her basket of apples. "Let me get that for you."

"I can handle it."

"Believe me—I know you can. I feel like doing something nice for you. Is that okay?" He winked and left his hand out.

Grams blushed and handed the basket to Luke before turning to Amy. "What did I tell you? A keeper!"

"Well, this keeper needs to eat," Amy said.

"I saved his plate of food. We'll warm it up real quick." She pointed to the basket of apples. "And I'm going to make a fresh apple crumb pie later for our special guest."

"Why not bring one from the shop?"

"No way," Grams said. "Those pies are for sale. I want to make one especially for Luke, one with extra love."

"Thank you kindly," Luke said.

A tow truck rumbled by with Nathan's truck attached to the back. Greg and Nathan approached and watched as the truck drove off the property and disappeared.

"My truck," Nathan mumbled to himself, still looking off into the distance, even though the tow truck was long gone. A few seconds later he turned and glared at Luke. "This is all your fault."

"What are you talking about?" Amy asked, stepping toward Nathan. "Don't you try to blame this on Luke. He wasn't the one driving your truck."

"Amy, please stay out of this."

"I've got this," Luke said, pulling Amy back. "Why don't you tell *me* what you're talking about. How is this my fault?"

"You spooked Dip Shit when you came up from behind us on Stardust," Nathan said. "I had everything under control until you showed up."

Luke stifled a laugh. "Everything under control?"

"That's right."

Luke nodded. "You're saying I spooked Dip Shit even though I wasn't even moving? And who was the one revving his engine and taunting Dip Shit? Maybe I should be asking who the real Dip Shit is here."

"Enough," Greg said, putting up his hand to silence them. "What's done is done, but it's obvious Luke has a problem with following directions. I told you we didn't need your help."

"Seriously, Dad?" Amy said. "He's the only one who seems to get things done around here! You should thank him."

"I'm going to agree with Amy," Grams said. "Give the boy a break."

"Come on, Luke." Amy grabbed his hand. "You need to eat something."

He would be happy to skip a meal if he could keep holding Amy's hand. He loved how she defended him, too. It wasn't an act. She was a good person with a good heart. Her dad, on the other hand, had issues that needed to be dealt with. But Luke was on the man's property, so he would let it slide and get something in his stomach.

Amy squeezed Luke's hand as they walked to the house.

Damn.

There was that urge to kiss her again.

"Fine," Greg called out from behind. "You go eat, even though we're short-handed around here, and the stalls haven't been mucked. Nathan can take care of it."

Luke pulled Amy to a stop and turned around. "I'd be happy to help."

"No," Amy said. "Let it go. You need to eat." She pulled Luke, but he wasn't budging.

"This won't take long," Luke said.

Yes, he was hungry, but Amy paid him to do a job and he would do it. And he wouldn't stop until Nathan was out of her life for good.

"There are eighteen stalls," Greg said, a challenge in his voice.

"Piece of cake," Luke said. "Three hours tops."

"I can do it in two and a half hours," Nathan said.

"Two hours and fifteen minutes," Luke said.

Greg's gaze popped back and forth between Luke and Nathan. "Well, well, boys. Sounds like we've got ourselves a little competition on our hands. Now you're talkin' my language. How about we make a little wager while we're at it? Luke takes the nine stalls on the left and Nathan takes the nine on the right. Let's see who's the fastest. And now for the wager."

"What?" Amy almost yelled. "You're going to bet money on cleaning up horse shit? You have lost your mind."

"Not money," Greg said. "I've got something better. The winner has dinner with you this evening."

Luke loved the direction of this conversation. That's all he wanted was to take Amy out. Away from the property for a few hours. Maybe there was a country bar or a dive they could go to and hang out. Heck, it didn't matter. They could even go back to town to eat in one of those pie shops. As long as he was alone with her. He knew Amy felt the same way but was still fighting it. Maybe she'd go along with the bet. Luke was certain he would win. He needed Amy to be okay with it.

"No!" Amy said. "I'm not going to be a prize in some ridiculous bet." Amy grabbed Luke's hand again and pulled him toward the house once again. "Come on, Luke. Now."

Luke slipped free from Amy's grip and took a couple of steps toward Nathan until they were face to face. "I'll take that bet." He held out his hand and waited.

"This is asinine," Amy said. "And it's *not* happening. Do you hear me?"

Nathan grabbed Luke's hand and shook it, while adding another failed attempt to squeeze juice out of it. "You're on."

"You're all crazy," Amy said. "And Luke hasn't had a thing to eat today. That's not fair at all."

"Go ahead and eat!" Greg said, looking like he was enjoying every bit of this. "Eat all you want. When you're done meet us over at the stalls. Say, in an hour? That will give you time for seconds and thirds. Hell, eat all the food in the kitchen. That sounds more than fair."

"No," Amy said.

"Yes," Luke said. "I'll be there in one hour." He grabbed Amy's hand and this time he was the one pulling toward the house, with Grams right behind them. "Don't worry. I've got this."

"My money is on Luke," Grams said, following close behind as they entered the kitchen.

"Is my darling betting again?" Grandpa Leo asked. "I know you gambled once when you took a chance on me, but what is it this time?"

Amy sighed. "Dad came up with some crazy idea for Luke and Nathan to have a stall-mucking competition. Luke takes the stalls on the left and Nathan takes the stalls on the right."

"I've got my money on Luke, too! Who's the bookie?" Grandpa Leo said.

"This isn't a joke," Amy said. "Plus, Nathan would have an unfair advantage since two of the stalls on the right haven't been used in over a year. They're clean, which means he would only have to clean seven instead of nine. That's why he gave you the left side."

"I'm not worried about it," Luke said, setting the basket of apples on the kitchen counter.

"Well, *I* am."

"If you're so worried why did you agree to going out with the winner?"

Amy blinked. "Were you not listening out there? I didn't agree to anything! There's no way I would accept the terms."

"You don't want to go out with me?"

"I don't want to go out with Nathan."

Luke grinned. "Odds are in my favor, you know."

Amy placed her hands on her hips. "You don't get it. Even if the odds were one in a million that he could win, there's still a possibility he could win. I'm not willing to take that chance."

Luke pulled Amy close and kissed her on the forehead.

Man, he loved doing that.

That shut her up, too.

Amy glanced at Luke's lips and hesitated. "What . . . was that for?"

"You're damn cute when you're trying to be upset."

"Trying to be? I *am* upset."

"Well, you don't have to worry about going out with Nathan. It'll be you and me this evening. Have a little faith. Besides, I saw the stalls when we were putting Stardust away. They didn't look bad and I have a foolproof technique guaranteed to help me win."

"I'll be back in a jiffy," Grandpa Leo said.

"Where are you off to with that mischievous look on your face?" Grams asked, grabbing Luke's plate and sticking it in the microwave. "You're up to something."

"Who me?" Grandpa Leo said. "I need to take care of a few things—that's all." He winked and went back outside, whistling on the way.

Amy turned to Grams. "What is he up to?"

Grams poured a glass of orange juice and placed it on the table in front of Luke. "Up to something, that's for sure. But whatever it is, I know he's doing it for the right reason."

CHAPTER THIRTEEN

Luke walked to the stables with a happy, full stomach. Even heated up in the microwave, the breakfast hit the spot as he washed it down with two cups of coffee and a glass of fresh-squeezed orange juice. He was charged up and ready to go with the next task of the day.

He had to admit mucking stalls had never entered his mind when he had signed up to help Amy, but all was good. He'd always felt right at home on a ranch. Anywhere in the country or in nature. He wasn't knocking city life, because it wasn't such a bad place either. Plus, it was where he had met Amy.

Luke smiled at the thought of Amy trying to talk him out of mucking the stalls. He'd already decided, though. He would put Nathan and her dad in their places. It was the right thing to do, but he was doing it for Amy. She accused him of being more stubborn than Baa Baa and he wouldn't argue that, because she was right.

Especially when it came to doing something for the woman in his life.

Wait a minute.

What was going on in Luke's mind?

Is she the woman in my life?

How had his thoughts gone there when they hadn't even been on a single date? Maybe it was because he could picture the two of them together, a better match than ribs and coleslaw. They had a lot in common. Probably even more than he knew, if she would let him get closer. The two of them together for a few hours would change that. He wanted to know everything about Amy. What was she afraid of? What made her happy?

Luke wanted to make her happy.

Right now, he needed to focus on kicking Nathan's butt by mucking the stalls. Then he could turn his attention back to the woman who was always on his mind.

"I was beginning to think you weren't going to show up," Greg said as Luke approached the stables.

Amy's dad must surely need relief from whatever was stuck up his ass.

Luke stopped and checked his watch, sure he wasn't late. "You said an hour, and it's been an hour."

"Well, I said you could take an hour, but I didn't expect you to use all of it."

Luke glanced over at Nathan who was leaning against the post. He hadn't changed his clothes, which was odd. Luke had changed out of his flannel shirt and into a t-shirt. Ruben was kind enough to let him borrow rubber boots. Better safe than sorry when it came to mucking.

Greg clapped his hands. "Let's get started. All the horses

are already in the pasture. All you have to do is choose your weapons." He pointed over at the tools against the stable wall. A couple of wheelbarrows, pitchforks, gloves, broad shovels, and stable brooms. It was more than he needed.

Luke grabbed a pair of gloves and then put a pitchfork and a broom in one of the wheelbarrows.

Greg gestured to the stalls. "Luke takes the nine stalls on the left and Nathan takes the nine on the right. Manure and wet bedding go over there." He pointed to an open area. "Questions?"

Luke kept his mouth shut, preferring to get this done and over with.

"Fine." Greg swung the gate open that led to the stables. "What are we waiting for? Go!"

Nathan didn't waste any time, cutting in front of Luke, banging into the side of his wheelbarrow and knocking it over. "Sorry about that." He grinned and continued into the stables.

"Not a problem," Luke said, righting his wheelbarrow and sliding the pitchfork and broom back inside. A ten-second delay wasn't going to make a difference at all.

Nathan flew past the first two stalls since they were spic and span, entering the third.

Amy was right.

Once again, Luke wasn't worried about it one bit.

He placed the wheelbarrow close to the first stall door, turning it around so it was facing the direction he wanted to go when it was full. Then he entered the stall and pulled out the feed tubs, water buckets, and stall toys. Next, he grabbed the pitchfork and removed the manure and soiled bedding, piling it onto the wheelbarrow. He scraped the unsoiled bedding to one side so it could be reused and then swept, piling the rest of the remnants on top of the wheelbarrow. After emptying the wheelbarrow he used it to grab fresh bedding and moved it back inside the stall, spreading it around evenly across the stall floor to replace what he had removed. After sweeping up the doorway and making sure everything was perfect and knocking down a few spiderwebs with the broom, he moved on to the second stall, but not before glancing over in Nathan's direction to see how far he had gotten.

Nathan was still in the same stall, grunting and already breathing heavy. His wheelbarrow was only half full, which was a good sign.

Luke continued the same process, picking up speed with each stall he cleaned. The closer he got to catching up with Nathan, the faster he worked. Even with the head start that Nathan had gotten, Luke was confident he could still win.

Almost an hour later, Luke had almost caught up with Nathan. That's when he pictured his date with Amy. The two of them, holding hands, talking intimately about life, kissing . . . Still, he needed to focus and get his head back in the game, because he wasn't finished yet. He picked up the pace even more because Nathan was finishing up his second-to-last stall and getting ready to move to his last.

Nathan entered his last stall to clean and froze. "Shit!"

Luke minded his own business and kept his head down, working even faster.

"What the hell did this horse eat?" Nathan called out, his voice raising an octave even more frustrated. "Holy hell, I can't breathe!"

Luke chuckled, hoping the longer Nathan talked and complained, the slower he would work. He finished the stall and made his way to the last one, knowing it would be a close race.

"I'm dying in here!" Nathan said, piling manure onto the wheelbarrow. He emptied the wheelbarrow and then returned to fill it again. "How can this be? This is not possible!" There was a loud thump, then a bang, like the wheelbarrow had hit the stall wall. "Ahhhh!"

Luke held in a laugh and moved to the next stall.

Last one.

He placed the wheelbarrow close to the door, turning it around one last time so it was facing the direction he wanted to go when it was full. Then he entered the stall and pulled out the feed tubs, water buckets, and stall toys as he had done with the other stalls.

"This is not fair," Nathan called out. "Not fair at all."

Luke grabbed the pitchfork and removed the manure and soiled bedding, piling it onto the wheelbarrow. He scraped the unsoiled, clean bedding to one side, swept, and piled the rest of the remnants on top of the wheelbarrow.

Almost there. Keep pushing.

Luke emptied the wheelbarrow, grabbed fresh bedding and moved it back inside the stall, spreading it around evenly across the stall floor. All he needed to do was a little more sweeping around the doorway and he was done.

"What are you complaining about?" Greg said, showing his face for the first time since they had started the competition. He entered Nathan's last stall and froze. "Holy hell! Where did all this shit come from?"

"I have no idea! Did you have an elephant in here?"

Luke thought of what Grandpa Leo had said in the kitchen earlier.

I need to take care of a few things.

Luke held in another laugh and shook his head, thinking of how a ninety-year-old man could have moved all that crap into Nathan's last stall in such a short amount of time.

"What are you doing sitting in it?" Greg asked.

"I fell!" Nathan said.

"Well, get yourself up and keep working or you'll lose. Is that what you want?"

"No, but look at this stall."

"Quit looking and keep going. You need to finish the job before Luke—"

"All done," Luke called out, pulling off his gloves and throwing them in the wheelbarrow.

"That can't be," Greg said, entering Luke's stall and looking around. He huffed and then went back and entered every one of the other stalls that Luke had cleaned, looking more shocked and frustrated with each clean stall he looked at.

Finally, Greg came out of the last stall and approached Luke, stopping and crossing his arms. "You cheated."

Luke stared at him. "What? How did I cheat?"

He pointed to Nathan's last stall. "You had something to do with that, didn't you?"

"To do with what?"

"The amount of shit in that stall."

Luke chuckled. "You're insane if you think I went in there, dropped my pants, and made *that* happen."

"You know what I mean," Greg said.

"No. I don't. I was eating breakfast and I wasn't alone. You saw me arrive and the only thing I did was muck the stalls as I was told. I finished before Nathan. Fairly. I'm going out with Amy tonight, which is the way it should be since she's my fiancée." Luke took a few steps toward the house, then stopped and turned around. "And why would you want Amy to go out with her ex, anyway?"

Greg flared his nostrils. "Nathan is a good man, and he comes from a good family. I know what's best for my daughter."

"All due respect, sir, your daughter is smart enough to know who and what is best for her, and she has already decided that Nathan is not it." He glanced over at Nathan, who was scraping horse manure off his jeans. "No offense."

"None taken," Nathan said. "But you're right, and I'm tired of this shit." He looked around the stall. "Not *this* shit that I'm covered in, although this hasn't been fun, either. I'm talking about putting my life on hold and waiting for Amy. I don't know what I was thinking. Well, I know what I was thinking." He turned to Greg. "Sorry. The deal's off."

Luke's gaze bounced back and forth between Greg and Nathan. "What deal?"

Greg cleared his throat. "Nothing." He pointed to Nathan. "We need to talk. Now. My office."

Nathan shook his head. "No. It's over. Amy has moved on and it's about time I do the same. The best man won." He pulled off his glove and offered his hand to Luke. "Congratulations."

Luke shook Nathan's hand. "Thank you—I appreciate it." He patted him on the back. "And you'll meet someone new who will appreciate you for who you are." He glanced down at Nathan's clothes. "Shower before you meet her, though, if you know what I mean."

Nathan chuckled. "Yeah . . . Good call." He glanced over at the main house. "Tell Amy I wish her the best."

"Don't do this," Greg said. "Not now."

"The deal's off."

Greg stood there, his face getting redder and redder as Nathan walked away.

"You have no idea what you've done," Greg said to Luke. "You've ruined everything."

"I have no idea what kind of a scheme you had going with Nathan, but it didn't benefit either of them," Luke said. "How can you wish misery on your daughter? And what about Nathan? The only thing I did was help give Amy some closure on something she was trying to forget about for years. I didn't ruin anything. You wanted me to muck stalls and I did, but it backfired on you."

Luke turned and walked toward the house, wondering what "the deal" was between Nathan and Greg. It sure sounded like it involved Amy and he would ask her about it when they were on their date. As for the moment, a nice hot shower would do him good. He mucked those stalls almost twice as fast as he normally had in the past and he was feeling soreness and tightness in his muscles.

"Hey, cowboy," Jennie said, walking through the gate with a bag of groceries. "What are you up to?"

"Fun stuff, you know . . . mucking stalls and all that." He pointed to her grocery bag. "Need help with that?"

"Nah—I'm good." Jennie eyed his biceps and hands. "Looks like you got a good workout."

Luke nodded. "Yeah. Looking forward to a hot shower."

"Well, the water is turned off at the moment. There's a plumber working on something."

"Oh. Did they say how long it would be?"

Jennie shook her head. "No, but if you don't want to wait

around, go jump in the hot springs."

Luke had heard that hot springs were therapeutic but had never been in one.

There was one problem.

"I didn't bring trunks," he said.

Jennie laughed. "Silly. You don't wear anything when you go in. It's private out there, so nobody will bother you. Grab a towel and a change of clothes and follow the flagstone path past the big oak tree. You can't miss it. We'll be in the kitchen when you're done."

A soak in the hot springs sounded much better than a shower. Luke grabbed a shower towel from the guest house bathroom and a fresh change of clothes, and then made his way up the flagstone path, past the big oak tree to the hot springs.

It was secluded and private as Jennie had mentioned. The sound of the water bubbling and the sight of the steam rising into the air made it look so inviting. He couldn't wait to get in.

Luke stripped off his clothes and stepped into the water, finding a place to sit. He closed his eyes and sighed, marveling at the fact that the hot springs were all natural.

This was nature at its finest.

This was heaven.

Twenty minutes in the water should be enough to relax his muscles. Then he would find Amy in the kitchen and plan their date for this evening.

Too bad she couldn't join him in the hot springs at that moment.

Right. Dream on.

Like that would ever happen.

CHAPTER FOURTEEN

Amy peeled and cut apples in the kitchen, trying to keep her mind off the stables. Nathan and Luke had decided to go ahead with the stall mucking competition even though she'd objected to such a childish activity.

Still. She hoped Luke won.

Jennie entered the kitchen, out of breath. "I'm in trouble. We need to talk."

Amy set the knife down on the cutting board and wiped her hands. "What happened?"

Jennie shook her head. "Not here. We need privacy."

Amy hesitated. "Okay. Where?"

"The hot springs."

"Now?"

"Yes. Now."

Amy loved her niece to bits, but still didn't trust her after the stunt she'd pulled at the Double Deuce. Sure, it ended up working out because Amy had met Luke and hired him to help get Nathan out of her life and to get her dad off her back, but still . . .

"Can't it wait? Amy asked. "What's going on?"

Jennie sighed. "It's of a romantic nature and no, it can't wait. Look—it's a long story, but I know you can help me. I need you, plus the water will relax me and I need to relax. Please say yes. I can't handle more rejection."

Rejection?

Amy would help Jennie in any way possible.

Family always came first.

Unless it was her father.

"Okay," Amy said, with as much enthusiasm as she could muster up, which wasn't much at all. "Give me two minutes to change and grab a towel. And tell Grams the apples are peeled and ready."

A few minutes later Amy headed down the flagstone path with Jennie toward the giant oak tree. A dip in the hot springs would be an even better distraction since she'd been in the kitchen wracking her brain over what to do with Luke. Well, she wasn't going to do *anything* with him. But the problem was she'd thought about doing *something* with him, more than a few times. And that something may or may not have been a little naughty.

But she had to stay strong.

He was a cowboy.

Cowboys were off limits.

Maybe it would be a different story if she were ten years younger and he wasn't a cowboy.

Then again, maybe not.

"Oh, crap," Jennie said, stopping halfway up the path and touching the back of her head.

Amy stopped. "What happened?"

"I need to run back to my room. I forgot my scrunchy. I can't get my hair wet since I had it colored. Get in the water. I'll be right there."

Amy nodded. "Okay." She watched Jennie walk back toward the main house and then turned back toward the hot springs, taking in a deep breath of fresh air. There was nothing like being in the country.

The sounds.

The smells.

The tranquility.

The naked man.

Amy stopped and jerked her head back.

Oh. My. God.

Luke was coming out of the hot springs, dripping wet, and buck naked as the day he was born.

Don't look down. Keep your eyes up. Up!

Too bad her mind wouldn't listen.

Amy swallowed hard. "Uh . . ."

The word was supposed to be silent, but it slipped out.

"Sorry!" Luke saw Amy for the first time, appearing just as shocked as her. He grabbed the towel and tied it around his waist, covering his manly attributes.

Amy was frozen.

Luke stood frozen, a slow smile growing on his face

They were like two giant human popsicles.

Luke glanced over at his clothes sitting on the bench near the oak tree. "Sorry."

Don't be.

"Jennie told me there wouldn't be anyone else here."

Amy glanced back down the hill toward the main house, then swung back around toward Luke. "Jennie told you to come here?"

"More like convinced, but yeah . . ."

"You're kidding."

Luke grabbed his shirt off the bench and pulled it over his head. "I was going to shower in the guest house, but she said they were working on a plumbing problem. I hope this is okay."

"It's always okay to use the hot springs, but we've both been taken for a ride."

"What do you mean?"

"Jennie also convinced me to come here. Then she said she had to get something from her room, but something tells me she won't be coming back."

Luke chuckled. "Have I told you that you have an interesting family?"

"Interesting is not the word I would have chosen."

"If you turn around for a second, I can slip my pants on," Luke said.

"Oh . . ." She glanced down at the towel wrapped around his waist.

Amy flipped around and faced the oak tree, waiting for Luke to put his pants on. She should have known her mind would wander. She could picture him dropping the towel and grabbing his silky boxers. Then his pants. She didn't have to use her imagination about what he had underneath it, because she had already seen it all, and it was difficult to get that image out of her mind.

"There," Luke said. "You can turn around now."

Amy turned back around and glanced down at the jeans he was now wearing, not sure what to say next.

Luke glanced at Amy's body, then opened his mouth and closed it.

"What?" Amy said.

"It's just . . . Jennie said nobody ever wears anything when they come in here, so I'm surprised you've got a bikini on. Not that I mind or anything."

"I told you—we were duped. She wanted you to be naked here when I arrived. Not sure what she thought that would lead to. I was supposed to have a soak."

Luke gestured to the steamy water. "Don't let me stop you."

Amy wasn't going to drop her towel and get in the water in front of him. Sure, she may have had a dream or two about doing that exact thing, his wanting eyes on her, but it was a dream.

This was a reality and it wouldn't happen.

Not with anyone who resembled, talked, or acted like a cowboy.

"Thanks, but I've changed my mind," Amy said. "I have no idea what possessed my niece to do this."

Luke laughed. "She had the best of intentions."

"I don't understand where these intentions are coming from and why she's motivated to get us together."

Luke shrugged. "Maybe she knows something we don't know."

Amy snorted. "And what would that be?"

"I don't know . . . Maybe we're a good fit."

Amy didn't respond.

THERE'S SOMETHING ABOUT A COWBOY

"I guess you never know, do you?"

No, you don't.

Luke was sexy as hell. He was kind and compassionate. She was attracted to him. She'd been denying it all along, but it was the truth.

"No comment?" Luke asked.

"About what?"

"About us."

Amy caught herself glancing at his chest again even though he had a shirt on now. She wanted to slap herself into another galaxy far, far away.

The bottom of Luke's lip curled up. "Well, anyway, I'm looking forward to our date this evening."

"There is no—"

"I know," Luke said. "There is no us. There is no date. You didn't agree to the bet. And Nathan and I are stubborn, stubborn men."

"You got that right." Amy crossed her arms. "You won then?"

He grinned.

She nodded and couldn't help letting a smile form on her lips. "Somehow I thought you would win. It won't end there, you know. Be prepared for more. My father and Nathan won't give up."

"What if I told you they already had?" Luke said. "Well, Nathan did."

"Did what?"

"Give up."

Amy blinked. "No way."

"Yes way," Luke said.

"You mean, *completely* gave up?"

He nodded. "Yes, ma'am."

"How do you know for sure?"

"The words came from Nathan's mouth. He also told me to tell you he wishes you the best."

Amy stared at Luke. "He said that?"

Luke nodded.

"Nathan?"

"Nathan. You're free. And you're welcome."

Before Amy could stop herself she lunged forward, wrapping her arms around Luke and squeezing him tight. "Thank you. You have no idea how much this means to me."

"I might . . ." He glanced down at her lips.

She glanced up at his, then caught herself and pulled away from his arms.

Amy cleared her throat and sat down on the bench in front of the oak tree, almost in shock. "Okay, I need to know everything."

"There's not much to tell." Luke sat on the bench next to her. "We mucked, he sucked, and you're a lucky duck." Amy laughed. "Nathan even shook my hand and said the best man won. And in case you're wondering who that is, it's me."

What was it with this man? This cowboy? It was like everything he touched turned to gold.

He knew how to get to her heart.

People say the nice guy always finished last, but in Amy's book—in her heart—the nice guy would always finish first. She'd never needed any macho alpha man who would throw her over his shoulder and make her a woman. She was already a woman. She didn't need some man to save her, either. She could take care of herself. Didn't need a man who would try to change her. She was picky and opinionated and she didn't see anything wrong with that. She wanted someone who would let Amy be Amy.

Luke was all those things.

Why wouldn't Amy give him a chance? Was it the age difference? She was beginning to believe it wasn't.

Maybe the problem wasn't dating cowboys.

Maybe the problem was dating *the wrong* cowboy.

Luke pointed to Amy's head. "You're thinking a lot. You almost done?"

Had she mentioned how smart and intuitive he was?

"Yeah," Amy said, tucking hair behind one ear. "It's a girl thing. We do that."

Luke chuckled. "Believe me, I know it's a girl thing, but you're cute when you do it. I don't mind." He nodded. "*So* darn cute. Anyway, you've been avoiding the topic. I think we need to get back to it. Our date."

Amy shook her head. "You never give up."

"Not if it's something I believe in."

"And you believe in going out on a date with me?"

"I believe that you're someone I want to get to know better," he corrected. "And that would require us spending time together on a date. Unless you want to give Nathan another shot."

"Not funny."

"Okay," Luke said. "You've got me."

How could she keep saying no to a man who she thought was perfect? How could she say no to a man she wanted to kiss again so badly?

"There you go thinking again. I will tell you what I was thinking, if you don't mind."

Amy didn't respond, knowing he would continue.

"I will give you the chance to pick what we do. Hopefully, you're not one of those types who thinks the man has to plan everything because it's romantic that way. I don't think you are."

He gets me so much it's scary.

"No," Amy said. "I mean, I like when a man surprises me occasionally, but I also like to plan things and surprise him. Or when we come up with something to do together."

"Perfect then. I thought I'd give you some options and let you decide since you're a big fan of rules. Here are your three options for this evening. For our date." He grinned, and she felt her heart banging in her chest. That cowboy's smile was deadly.

"Okay," Amy said. "Let's hear it."

"Karaoke."

Amy laughed. "Seriously?"

"Yup, but food and drinks first."

"That's what you came up for our first date? Karaoke?"

"I heard you singing in the kitchen when I walked by earlier. You have a beautiful voice. I want to hear more."

It was true she was singing in the kitchen. She loved singing, especially while she baked. Had been doing it since she was a little girl. And she loved karaoke too, but never on a first date. She rarely sang in front of a man she was interested in until they had gone out at least a few times.

Amy froze.

She was interested in Luke.

Her mind told her.

Amy's heart was now banging in her neck.

She felt her cheeks heating up.

Luke pointed to her face. "Care to share what's on your mind?"

"No," Amy said, preferring to change the subject. "What are my other two choices for the date tonight?"

"I'm glad you asked. A long walk on the beach."

"The nearest beach is ninety minutes away. You know that."

"A long walk by the lake."

Amy shook her head.

"What about a river? There's got to be a river close by."

Amy didn't even respond this time.

"We could do circles around a puddle? There's got to be a puddle around here somewhere. Grab a hose. We'll make one."

Amy laughed and playfully shoved him. "Okay, you're not taking this seriously."

Luke grabbed her hand. "I'm just having fun. It doesn't matter what we do. I want to spend time with you. It'll be fun."

She glanced down at her hand in his, her pulse once again racing. "Okay. Fun is good." She was having difficulty speaking. "What's the third option?"

He squeezed her hand. "Pie. At one of the places in town."

"No," she said, not hesitating. "Not an option."

He grinned. "Then karaoke it is."

She pulled her hand out of his. "You did that on purpose. You knew I would say no to pie, and the walk on the ocean was ridiculous. You like karaoke that much?"

"I've never done it."

"Never?"

"Never, ever."

She studied him for a moment. "You could fail miserably."

"You should know me by now. Failure is not an option. I'll keep doing it and doing it until I get it right."

"Sounds like you could be in for a long night."

Luke grabbed her hand again. "That's what I'm hoping for."

CHAPTER FIFTEEN

Luke grabbed Amy's hand and pulled her toward the front door of the Julian Pie Company on Main Street. "I'm in the mood for some pie. How about you?"

He was sure she would try to resist, but it was worth a shot.

She pulled her hand free and continued down the sidewalk. "Behave and keep moving, mister." She held up the bag in her hand. "We need to drop these off."

Amy had baked cookies earlier and Luke had promised she could drop them off at the nursing home downtown before their date. How could he say no to such a sweet thing?

"Be right back," Amy said, entering the nursing home. A few minutes later she came back out and smiled. "All done."

"That was fast."

"I told them I couldn't stay long because I had a date and they told me to have fun while I was young. Then they kicked me out. Can you believe that?"

"Remind me to go back and thank them." He grinned,

and then gestured to Mom's Pie House as they approached it. "This looks like a great place."

"No." She kept moving.

He pointed across the street. "Hey, look, Apple Alley Bakery. Pie, anyone?"

Amy didn't even look. "No."

He laughed again. "Fine. I'll give it a rest for now, if you slow down. Where should we eat dinner?"

Amy stopped and turned around, being a good sport about his joking around. "We have plenty of great places to eat around here." She wiggled her nose like a rabbit. "That smells good, wherever it's coming from."

"Smells like good old-fashioned barbecuing." He pointed to the rustic building on the corner. "Looks like it's coming from over there."

Amy didn't hesitate, crossing the street toward Main Street Grub & Pub. "What are we waiting for? Let's get a move on."

There were at least twenty people waiting outside under the awning which was a good sign.

"You ever been there?" Luke asked, as he was usually in the habit of checking reviews online before trying a new restaurant.

Amy shook her head. "Never heard of it. They had to have opened in the last year. They must be doing something right. Looks like we found our place for dinner."

"Just like that?"

Amy smiled. "Just like that."

They walked past the patio where smoke from the grill billowed over the fence.

Luke inhaled and nodded his appreciation. "Yup. Someone's grilling up something serious on the barbecue." They squeezed through the people waiting outside, then he swung the door open and waved Amy through. "After you."

"Thank you."

Luke entered behind Amy and stopped next to her, admiring the inside of the huge restaurant that was packed with people.

"I have a good feeling about this place." Luke glanced down at the wide plank wood floor and then up at the wooden beam ceiling. In fact, there was wood everywhere, including the long oak bar that traveled the length of the place on the left. It was as rustic inside as it was outside. An older man was seated on a stool in the middle of the stage to the right, playing the banjo and singing. "Live music, too. I like it."

"Me, too." Amy followed his gaze, then cranked her head around to look at the people waiting. "Although it could be awhile before we get a table."

"Maybe we'll get lucky."

"How many?" The man behind the counter kept his head down and scratched his chin, analyzing the wait list on his clipboard like he was in the middle of a complex sudoku puzzle.

"Two," Luke said. "Ocean view, if possible."

Amy laughed and nudged Luke with her elbow.

"The best I can offer is a fountain view in the back patio. Should be about forty-five minutes to an hour." The man looked up and stared at Luke. "You look familiar."

"Luke Jenkins!" someone called out from behind.

Luke swung around to the side and jerked his head back. "Emilio!" He lunged forward and hugged him. "I can't believe my eyes. What are you doing here?"

Emilio gestured around the restaurant. "This is my place. I

opened it nine months ago." He pointed to the man with the clipboard. "This is my brother, Miguel."

"What an honor." Miguel held out his hand. "I knew I recognized you from somewhere. I'm a big fan, even though you smoked my brother on national television."

Emilio placed his hands on his hips. "Smoked? I'd say he squeaked by with a win."

Luke chuckled and shook Miguel's hand. "A pleasure to meet you, but I agree with Emilio. A different set of judges and he could've beaten me."

Emilio slapped Luke on the back. "You're way too kind." He gestured to Amy. "And this lovely lady must be your fiancée."

Luke turned to Amy, his mouth hanging open. "Uh . . ."

Was he supposed to pretend they were engaged when they were in public, too? Or was it in front of her family? They hadn't discussed that. And how did Emilio find out?

Emilio pointed to the ring on Amy's finger. "Come on. You can't hide that from me."

Amy held up her hand and stared at the ring. "Oh—that. Guilty!" She laughed. "I'm Amy." She smiled and shook Miguel and Emilio's hands.

Well played.

"Emilio!" someone shouted.

Emilio gestured over his shoulder with his thumb. "Looks like I need to get back to the kitchen, but I want to catch up with you. I'll stop by your table later. Are they already on the wait list?"

"Not yet," Miguel said, handing Emilio the clipboard.

"Let's see." Emilio checked out the list and the table chart, then glanced toward the tables. He handed the clipboard back to Miguel. "Give them table fourteen. Dinner's on us this evening. And congratulations on your engagement."

Miguel showed Amy and Luke to a cozy booth in the corner, then placed two menus in front of them. "You heard my brother. Order whatever your hearts desire. Our treat. Do you like beer?"

"Yes," Luke and Amy said together.

"Great. I'll send over a flight sampler. Four of our best beers. Enjoy."

"Thanks," Amy and Luke said together again.

Amy watched Miguel walk back to the front of the restaurant. "What are the chances?"

"It's crazy," Luke said. "Emilio is from Costa Rica, but I met him in Florida during the taping of *Barbecue Pitmasters*. He worked his butt off to get where he is today, I know that much. It's not a surprise he has his own restaurant. I don't understand how he ended up here in Julian, of all places."

Amy nodded. "It was a smart move on his part. This town may only have fifteen-hundred people, but tourism keeps it going and there are no other barbecue places for miles."

"Well, one thing is for sure . . . with Emilio as the chef, we're in for a real treat. I guess it was fate you chose this place. Kind of like how we met."

"Oh, you think that was fate?" Amy seemed to consider the possibility.

"Definitely fate. And I also think I have a solution to your little issue with me being a cowboy."

"Really?" She squished her eyebrows together, not looking convinced at all. "What are you going to do? *Un*cowboy yourself?"

"I am. From this day forward, I'm a gladiator."

Amy burst with laughter. "A gladiator . . ."

Luke nodded. "Call me General Maximus."

"Okay—that won't work because I may have had one or two Russell Crowe fantasies."

"There you go. That's fate again." Luke leaned closer, their lips inches apart. "Like it's fate we kissed right here in this booth."

"We didn't kiss in this—"

Luke's lips were on hers. He couldn't help himself. And just like that he was lost in their kiss. Amy wasn't resisting this time, wasn't complaining like she normally did, and that made him like her even more. She was kissing him back, and this was a kiss to remember.

He pulled away from the kiss. "See? Fate. I hope you're not going to disagree with me."

Amy hesitated, staring at his mouth. "Uh . . . no . . . I don't think I will."

"Good. Then I guess we should look at the menu before the waiter comes."

She nodded, licking her lips. "Great idea, but before we do that, there's one more thing." Amy leaned forward, yanked Luke by the neck, and kissed him good.

"Evenin', folks," the waiter said, clearing his throat. "Sorry to interrupt, but Miguel asked me to bring this over." He placed the flight of beer on the table. "Ready to order?"

Amy grabbed the menu and held it high, trying to cover the embarrassment on her face.

"We haven't even looked at the menu yet," Luke said. "We'll need a couple more minutes."

"Of course. Take your time."

A few seconds later Luke said, "You can come out now."

Amy lowered the menu and looked around. "I'm mortified. We need to control that."

"That was chemistry."

"That was embarrassing."

"It's not that big of a deal. I mean . . . we're two consenting adults—"

"Making out in a restaurant."

Luke chuckled. "Yeah—I guess we were. But if I want to make out with my fiancée, I'm going to make out with my fiancée. Who's going to stop me? Nobody, that's who."

Amy laughed. "I'll stop you, because I'm starving."

Luke nodded and grabbed one of the beer samples, handing it to her. "I'm starving too, but first a toast." He grabbed another sample and held it in the air. "To us."

Amy hesitated.

"We've got something here," Luke said. "Let it happen."

Let it happen.

He was right. One hundred percent right. She needed to quit fighting it.

She clinked his glass. "To us."

Amy took a sip of her beer, knowing she had stepped over to the other side, where feelings happened, relationships grew, and people fell in love. Now there was nothing she could do about it but hold on and enjoy the ride. She trusted Luke. It was obvious he was a good man, so what did she have to lose?

Her heart, that was all.

They ended up ordering and sharing a sampler plate of

ribs, chicken, links, and pulled pork. It was out of this world. Amy enjoyed every minute of the conversation. Now that she had let it happen, it was like a weight had been lifted off her shoulders. Everything fell right into place.

The waiter returned later with a dessert platter and placed it on the table in front of Amy and Luke. It was loaded with four slices of different styles of apple pie. "Here you go. A taste of Julian. Each award-winning pie is from a different baker right here in our downtown. If you're curious, their names are under each plate."

Amy studied the slices of pies on the platter and turned to Luke. "Do you ever take no for an answer?"

Luke threw up his palms. "I didn't order this."

The waiter gestured to the dessert. "This is compliments of Emilio. He said to enjoy it and he'll stop by to chat with you. Oh, and coffee is on the way."

Luke grinned.

Amy pointed to his face. "Don't say it."

"What?"

"You were going to say it was fate that Emilio sent over this pie."

He placed his hand on his chest. "Me?" His bottom lip quivered, and then he laughed. "Okay, maybe it was on my mind." He grabbed a fork and cut into the first slice, letting it hover in front of Amy's mouth. "Take a bite and tell me the ingredients."

She sat back. "What?"

"You told me you've dreamed of tasting the pies of your competitors and trying to figure out the exact ingredients they used. Now's your chance. And nobody's watching you, except for me." He held his fork close to her mouth again. "Come on. Open up."

She hesitated, but then leaned forward and took a bite of the pie from Luke's fork, chewing and nodding. "Wow. That's good."

Luke cut into the slice and took his own bite. "That *is* good. Now tell me what's in it."

Amy smiled and told him the ingredients.

Luke nodded. "Very impressive. Okay, try this one." He forked a little of the next slice and slid it slowly into Amy's mouth. Then he had a bite of his own. He glanced at her, a confused look on his face. "That was almost identical to the first one."

"They're similar, but this one had a little more butter. It might help if you cleanse your palate, like they do during wine tasting."

Luke took a sip of water and tried another bite. "Hmmm. A little more cinnamon, too."

"Very impressive, Mr. Gladiator."

"It's General Maximus, please." He looked around the restaurant. "Hmm. Have you seen my sword?"

Amy laughed. "Yes. At the hot spring. Very impressive." She threw her hand over her mouth.

Luke's mouth fell open.

I didn't just say that.

The temperature seemed to be going up in the restaurant.

Amy avoided eye contact and took a bite of the third slice, eager to change the subject. "Interesting . . . okay, tell me if you can figure out the magic ingredient in this one. It has something the other two don't have."

Luke took a bite and chewed. "Nutmeg."

"Yes!" She watched Luke for a moment. "How do you know so much about pie ingredients?"

"I've done my fair share of baking."

Amy laughed again. "Right."

"I'm serious."

Why had she doubted him? The man was a professional chef on the barbecue, but that didn't mean he couldn't bake. After all, the man was perfect. Amy felt bad.

She reached over and grabbed his hand. "Sorry. That was rude of me to assume you knew nothing about baking."

"That's okay."

"No. It's *not* okay. Tell me, what do you like to bake?"

"I can only bake two things. Coincidentally, one of them is pie. I told you I was a big fan and I wasn't lying. I used to help my grandma make pies almost every Sunday when I was a kid, and it kind of stuck with me over the years. It reminds me of her every time I take a bite."

Amy smiled. "That's sweet. And what's the other thing you bake?"

"Cornbread." He grinned. "Goes perfect with barbecue." He forked another bite of pie. "Are your pies better than these?"

She looked around to make sure nobody was listening, then leaned closer to him and whispered, "Yes, but these are fantastic. Like the waiter said, they've won awards."

"Have your pies won awards?"

"Yes. Well . . . not recently, but three years ago I won the Julian Pie Contest. I didn't enter the last two years."

Emilio slid into the booth next to Luke. "Sorry. Crazy night. I swear I can barely keep up." He blew out a deep breath and smiled. "Did you enjoy your dinner?"

"It was amazing," Amy said.

"I agree," Luke added. "That was some good eatin' there. Thank you."

"It was my pleasure." Emilio nudged Luke on the arm. "What about you? Where do you live and what have you been up to? We promised to keep in touch, but we haven't done a very good job."

"I know, I know. We need to work on that, but not much is happening with me at the moment. I still live in San Diego, but Amy's family lives here. We're visiting for the week."

"And work?"

"Work . . ." Luke chuckled. "Well, I'm looking for my next opportunity."

Emilio scratched his head. "You're kidding me. You're not working at the moment?"

"I wish I were. I met a couple of investors who had been thinking about buying the building next door to the Double Deuce and turning it into the premier barbecue restaurant in San Diego. But I haven't heard back from them. I think they got spooked when they found out how much capital was necessary to build a showcase open-air kitchen, which is what I wanted. You know how much it costs."

"I do, but they're worth every penny."

"That's what I told them, but I don't think they were listening. I was tempted to use the money I won in the competition to pay for it myself. I met with someone else who wanted to convert the Hillcrest Theater into a dinner theater, but that fell through, too. I've been getting offers, but nothing seems to be the right fit yet."

Emilio slapped Luke on the back. "I think fate brought you here, my friend."

Luke grinned and turned to Amy. "Did you hear that? Fate."

Amy shook her head. "I heard."

"We should talk," Emilio said. "I'm looking to do the exact same thing—I mean, expand next door. But I want to add a garden and eating space for weddings, plus a second kitchen for catering. I'm not looking for an employee, though. I'm looking for a partner. This is going to be big."

Luke sat up. "Seriously?"

Emilio nodded. "Promise me you won't leave town without talking with me."

"I promise."

"Great!" Emilio slid back out of the booth. "It was a pleasure meeting you, Amy."

"You, too," Amy said.

They watched Emilio walk away.

Luke turned to Amy and grinned.

She held up her index finger. "Don't say it."

"I wasn't going to say anything *at all*." He grinned. "Even though it was fate."

Amy pinched Luke on the arm. "I told you not to say it."

They shared a laugh as the banjo player on the stage stood. "Thank you, folks. Hope you enjoyed the music."

The people in the restaurant applauded.

"And now, it's karaoke time with DJ Victor! Take it away, Victor."

Amy blinked and turned to Luke again. "Did you plan this?"

Luke shook his head. "Nope. Just another case of—"

"Okay," DJ Victor said. "You heard him—it's karaoke time. Who's ready to sing?"

Luke slid out of the booth.

Amy sat up straight. "Where are you going?"

"You'll see." He walked toward DJ Victor.

"I hope you're signing yourself up because I'm not singing."

Luke ignored her and went up on stage. He talked to the DJ and then pointed back at Amy. The DJ nodded and gave Luke a thumbs-up.

Amy shook her head and mouthed *no*.

Luke replied with a wink and a smile.

Her pulse began to race. She didn't want to do karaoke, but she had a feeling she wasn't going to have a choice. Luke was too damn charming to say no to, plus she was going to be put on the spot. She couldn't back down in front of everyone.

"Okay!" DJ Victor said on the microphone. "We already have our first victim . . . I mean singer."

The people in the restaurant laughed.

"Please give a warm welcome to Amy who'll be singing 'Just a Kiss' by Lady Antebellum!" DJ Victor pointed at Amy. The entire restaurant turned to stare at her. "Come on up, Amy. Don't be shy."

She slowly slid out of the booth and walked up the stairs to the stage, poking Luke in the chest. "You're dead."

He chuckled. "At least I'm going to die with a smile on my face. And, hey—you're stepping outside your comfort zone. That's a good thing."

"I like my comfort zone because, oddly enough, it gives me comfort."

"You'll do fine. I'll be right here with you." He winked. "And this is our song, remember?"

Amy hesitated and grabbed the microphone from the DJ,

shaking her head. She glanced at the monitor in front of her showing the song title and group.

I can't believe I'm going to do this.

"Here we go," DJ Victor said, pressing a button and starting the song.

A few seconds later she was singing about fighting feelings and kissing in the moonlight.

She was sure she was horrible, although Luke's smile said otherwise.

Was he sincerely enjoying her butcher one of her favorite songs?

This was supposed to be their song and she wasn't doing it justice.

Wait a minute.

Their song.

That gave Amy an idea.

During the bridge, she pulled Luke over in front of the monitor, slapping the microphone in his hand. "Your turn. Finish the song, cowboy."

He looked surprised at first, but then grabbed Amy before she could walk away.

Luke held onto her hand and then, without looking at the monitor, started singing to her.

And his voice melted her on the spot.

Are you kidding me? He can sing, too?

Luke didn't let go of her hand, singing his heart out about waiting all of his life for her. Then he sang about kissing her. His eyes never left hers and she could've sworn he was looking deep down into her soul.

Amy felt it. The connection. His emotion.

Now, all she wanted to feel was his kiss.

"It's never felt so real," he sang, leaning toward her, making her knees weak.

Amy was getting lost in his eyes, his words . . .

When the song was over, he pulled her close and pressed his lips to hers.

The restaurant erupted in applause and cheers.

She pulled away slowly, grateful he was holding her up. "You're forgiven."

They walked hand-in-hand off the stage and Luke stopped her. "Sure you don't want to sing another song?"

"Not funny. And you'd better not mention that four letter word again."

"You mean the one that rhymes with date?"

"Yes. That one."

"The only way you'll get me to shut up now is if you kiss me again."

Amy glanced at his lips, wanting, craving more. "You got yourself a deal."

She leaned into him and—

"The deal!" Luke smacked himself on the forehead with his palm.

Amy blinked. "Pardon me?"

"I can't believe I didn't tell you. Well, I had planned on telling you, but—"

"Tell me what?"

"Nathan and your dad were in cahoots. They had a deal."

Amy tilted her head to the side. "What do you mean? What kind of deal?"

"I don't know, but I'm sure you were a part of it."

"How could I be part of a deal and not know about it?"

"I have no clue," Luke said. "All I know is . . . after I beat Nathan at stall mucking, he told your dad the deal was off."

The deal was off?

Amy didn't like the sinking feeling in her stomach. It sounded like Nathan and her dad were up to no good. But what could it have been? Yes, Luke had assured her that Nathan was out of her life, but she needed to know the truth. And she sure as hell would find out.

CHAPTER SIXTEEN

"Dad!" Amy entered the house, the door slamming a little harder than she had wanted. She was pissed off but didn't need to take it out on the house. Luke respected her decision of confronting her dad by herself and waited for her at the guesthouse. She'd had a wonderful date with "The Singing Gladiator" and looked forward to spending more time with him, but this couldn't wait any longer. She was going to get some answers from her dad and she was going to get them right now.

Amy checked the living room, but he wasn't there.

Next, she looked in the kitchen.

Nobody there, either.

"Dad? Where are you?"

Nothing.

He had to be in the house somewhere because his car was there.

Amy walked down the hallway, stopping in front of his closed office door.

Odd.

That door was never closed.

"Dad?" She knocked twice.

No answer.

She turned the handle and slowly pushed the door open, peeking inside.

Her dad was lounging on his leather recliner in the corner of the office. He took a sip of his drink—most likely his usual rum and Coke.

Amy placed her hands on her hips. "I was calling you."

"I know." He took another sip. "It's late and I'm tired. Can we do this tomorrow?"

"You know why I'm looking for you?"

Greg sighed and placed his drink on the table next to the recliner. "Of course I know. I didn't expect Luke to keep his trap shut."

She didn't like the way her dad looked. She was angry at him, but that didn't mean she wanted to see him that way. It was like he'd aged a few years in one day. His shoulders were slumped, his energy was low, and he avoided eye contact with Amy. Speaking of his eyes, they were glossy and bloodshot. Definitely not his first drink.

Greg shifted in the recliner. "Go to bed. We'll talk in the morning."

Amy shook her head. "I want to know about the deal."

"It doesn't matter."

"It matters to me."

"Nathan is gone—you and Luke made sure of that. End of story."

"*Not* end of story." Amy crossed her arms. "Why did you want so bad for me and Nathan to be together?"

"Nathan's a good man."

"And? What else? You're not telling me everything. Spill it."

He reached for his drink and—

"Stop drinking and listen to me."

He stared at the glass and then set it back down, turning to Amy and waiting.

"Do you miss Mom?" she asked.

"Of course, I miss her," Greg said. "What the hell kind of question is that?"

"Are you going to miss me when I'm gone?"

"Again, what the hell kind of question is that?"

Amy blew out a deep breath. "I'm trying to let you know that you're very close to losing your daughter. I've had enough. Your behavior is unacceptable and I'm not even sure you love me anymore."

"Are you serious?" Greg wobbled as he stood. "Of course, I love you."

"You have a funny way of showing it. We don't talk anymore. You criticize everything I do. You don't respect my decisions. I know there's a lot you're not telling me, including whatever that deal was with you and Nathan. You'd better tell me everything. I mean everything, or I'm out of here."

Amy hadn't meant to get herself so worked up, but she needed to know the truth. She should have said all of this a long time ago, but she kept letting it slide because of how her mom's death had affected her father. It was hard on him, but it was hard on her, too. Enough was enough.

The ball was in his court.

He was stubborn—like most men—but she hoped he would make the right decision and tell her everything.

He pointed to his glass on the table. "Can I have another sip now?"

She nodded and tapped her foot on the floor.

Greg sat back down on the recliner, downed the rest of his drink, and placed the glass back on the side table. Then he pointed to his desk. "Everything you need to know is there on the desk in the brown folder."

Amy stared at her dad for a moment, wondering what he was talking about, and then took a few steps toward the desk.

She picked up the folder and stared at the outside, wondering what was on the inside.

Greg gestured to it. "Open it."

Amy hesitated and then opened the folder, glancing at the first page. It was a spreadsheet with sales figures for the company: apple sales, pie sales, receipts, expenses, etc. Many of the numbers were in red. She had never handled any of the accounting for the company, but red was not good.

The company was losing money.

A lot of money.

She shot a quick look at her dad, who was staying quiet, and then returned her attention back to the document, flipping through the rest of the pages. They were just as bad.

She dropped the folder back on the desk and looked at her dad. "I don't get it. I thought business was good."

He shook his head. "It hasn't been for a while. Things were great after you won the last pie contest, but that was a long time ago. And you didn't enter the last two years, so . . ."

"You're blaming me for this?" She gestured to the folder.

"No. I'm not saying that." He picked up the empty glass and then set it back down. "The truth is I haven't been a hundred percent focused since your mom's death. I let the bills pile up, then the interest piled up on those bills since I used credit cards to pay for almost everything. Then with the increased apple competition, our sales for Pie in the Sky took a hit. I haven't had the energy to get out there like I used to, and the sales suffered even more."

"Do Grandpa and Grams know about this?"

He shook his head. "I didn't want to worry them."

"How come you didn't tell me?"

"I didn't want to worry you, either."

"Who *did* you tell? Anyone?"

Greg opened his mouth and closed it.

"No," Amy said, fearing she knew the answer. "Nathan?"

"He said he could help."

"How? How could *he* help? Is that what the deal was about?"

Her dad didn't answer.

"Tell me. Now."

Greg hesitated. "He said he had a sure-fire way of getting us out of this mess. He was talking about taking it national with his contacts. Costco. Target. Just about every supermarket on every corner. He outlined everything, and it sounded like an incredible opportunity to take the company to a level most companies will never see."

Amy was even more confused than ever.

She rubbed her forehead. "I don't get it. What does this have to do with the deal between you and Nathan?"

Greg hesitated again.

"Dad?"

"Can I at least get another drink?"

"No. Tell me. Now. What was the deal?"

Greg fidgeted with the button on his sleeve and then pointed to his recliner. "Maybe you should sit down."

"I'm fine right where I am." She glared at him, tapping her foot on the floor again.

He started fidgeting with his button again. "Okay . . . You have to remember that Nathan was going to make all our problems go away. And that was a very good thing."

"I understand that, but *what* was the deal?"

Greg shrugged. "He needed something in return obviously, and there was only one thing I had that he wanted."

Amy blinked twice. "Please don't tell me—"

He didn't answer.

"You were going to sell off your only daughter?"

"No! It wasn't like that. I truly believed you would be happy with Nathan. People go to those dating agencies and get set up all the time. What's the difference?"

"What's the difference? This wasn't a setup. It was like an arranged marriage and you were trying to force me into it." Amy paced back and forth. "This is unbelievable. You could have come to me. You could have told me."

"You're never here anymore."

"I'm never here anymore because you were always trying to get me back with Nathan! I have money saved up."

"I couldn't ask you to do that."

"Seriously? You can trade your only daughter, but my own money isn't good enough? That's what family is for. We stick together and work through our problems instead of selling off our children to the highest bidder. I'm not your prized cow. I can't believe this. I need to get some fresh air." She turned toward the door.

Greg sat back down. "I'm sorry. We could lose everything. You understand that?"

Amy stopped and flipped back around. "How bad is it? What will it take to turn everything around and get us back on track?"

"I'm guessing seventy-five thousand."

Amy swallowed hard. She'd been saving her money, but she didn't have that much available. She made a decent salary at the hotel, but a good chunk of her paycheck went to pay the mortgage on her house each month.

"Is the property being foreclosed on?" she asked.

"Not yet."

"Good. Then there's time. We *are not* going to lose everything. We'll figure something out."

Her dad smiled. "It's good to have you back, sweetie."

"I'm not back, Dad. I'm just trying to help."

"I know. I do miss you around here, though. I've missed you every single day, even though I didn't show it. Everyone misses you around here."

She didn't answer, even though she missed being home, too. She was still too upset with her dad to mention it.

"We need to brainstorm this and figure out some things," Amy said.

"Another income stream would help," he said. "And maybe a fresh approach to marketing the pies. But the easiest thing you could do for us is enter the pie contest again. That exposure is better than paid advertising. They've even upped the ante because this year's winner will be on television and that would turn everything around for us, I'm sure of it."

Amy had been so disconnected from the pie industry, disconnected from Julian and her family, that she hadn't even been thinking about the pie contest. Winning that contest three years ago was one of the highlights of her career.

"I know I've behaved like a fool," her dad continued. "I'm truly embarrassed about my behavior, but we should look on the bright side."

"There's a bright side to all this? Please, do tell."

"You have Luke, your fiancé."

She couldn't argue with that, even though he didn't know the word *fake* was part of the equation. Still, it was because of her dad's foolish behavior that she had hired Luke in the first place.

For a brief moment Amy wondered what it would be like if he were her real fiancé. She felt a warmth envelop her heart just thinking of it. Then she remembered what he had said.

If I had a fiancée I would worship the ground she walked on. I would give her everything I've got. Everything. And that includes lovin', touchin', and squeezin', for starters.

Amy was suddenly in the mood to be loved and touched and squeezed.

She needed to get back to the room, but not before she cleared up one more thing.

"I'm surprised Luke is still around, considering you've been treating him like crap ever since he got here. You owe him an apology."

Greg nodded. "You're right. I do. And he'll get one first thing in the morning. Promise."

"Good." Amy walked back across the office and kissed her dad on the cheek. "I love you, but I'm still pissed off at you."

"I know, sweetie, and I don't blame you. I hope you can forgive me."

Amy walked back to the guesthouse, feeling better after

confronting her dad. What he'd done was wrong, but all hope wasn't lost. This could be fixed.

Amy entered the guest house quietly, in case Luke had fallen asleep.

She closed the door behind her and froze.

Hey," Luke said, sitting on the couch in his silk boxers, reading.

She pointed to his underwear, trying to hide the fact that her heart rate had kicked into second gear. "This is not normal. Men don't just sit around reading in their silk boxers."

"I do." He grinned and set his Kindle down on the couch, exposing more of his chest and abs. "How did it go? Did your dad 'fess up?"

Amy nodded, trying to maintain eye contact. "Yeah . . ."

"Don't want to talk about it?"

She sighed. "Right now, all I want to do is take a hot shower and relax, but I'll give you a quick recap, if you want. You won't believe it."

"Try me."

Amy sat down on the couch next to Luke. The man must have taken a shower because he smelled amazing.

She leaned in to get one more whiff before she told him about the deal and—

"What are you doing?" Luke asked.

"What do you mean?"

He pointed to her face. "You wiggled your nose like a rabbit. You did it when we were on the street and smelled the barbecue and you did it again now. Are you sniffing me?"

"No!" she said, way too loud for being seated right next to him. "Maybe . . ." She cleared her throat, ready to change the subject. "Anyway, do you want to know about the deal or not?"

He chuckled. "Yes."

"Fine. Nathan had a plan to take our pies national. He has the connections to make it happen."

"Wow. That's huge."

Amy nodded. "And in exchange, Nathan would get—"

"You."

She stared at Luke for a moment. "Of course you know. Let me ask you something . . . do you know everything?"

"It wasn't that hard to figure out. I mean—look at you. You're gorgeous. Who wouldn't want you? I certainly do."

"You . . ."

"Want you."

Amy rubbed the back of her neck and looked away. Was it getting hot in there? Heat seemed to be radiating from her body. Or was it coming from his body? She glanced over at the fireplace for a distraction, then the dog painting on the wall, then the painting of the basket of apples. She could still feel his eyes on her, but he was quiet.

Waiting.

Wanting.

She needed a moment to process things and decide her next move.

Amy stood and pointed toward the bathroom, then turned and locked eyes with Luke. "I'm, uh, going to go take a shower."

"Sounds good . . ." Luke picked up his Kindle and winked at her. "I won't move a muscle."

"Okay then . . ." Amy barely squeaked the word out and then headed directly to the bathroom.

In the shower, she tried to forget about Luke's sexy wink, his sexy body, his sexy smell—hell, his sexy everything. She also tried to forget what he had said earlier.

Look at you. You're gorgeous. Who wouldn't want you? I certainly do.

So much for trying to forget.

Later, she stepped out of the shower and into a bathrobe, her mind still occupied with Luke. She had strong feelings for him. As she predicted earlier, she had stepped over to the other side and was on a clear path to falling in love.

And she was going to fall hard and fast.

But the most amazing part was she didn't care, and she wasn't scared. In fact, this was the most relaxed she'd been in a long time. Nathan was out of her life and she finally understood what was going on with her dad. She couldn't have done it without Luke.

Mr. Perfect.

Luke had told her in his truck on the way to Julian that it could be rewarding when a person stepped outside their comfort zone. He'd said it again at the restaurant before she sang the song.

She was ready to take that theory to another level.

Amy came out of the bathroom and leaned against the doorframe, very aware that her robe was short and she was showing plenty of leg. Would Luke notice?

He turned in her direction and eyed her from head to toe. Twice.

Then he opened and closed his mouth. Twice.

That answers that question.

"How was your shower?" Luke asked, finally able to speak.

She loosened the robe around her neck. "Hot."

He nodded, still watching her every move. "Hot is . . . good."

There was silence, but their eyes never left each other.

"Even hotter with a gladiator. Would you happen to know one?" She loosened the belt and let her robe slide to the floor.

Luke set the Kindle on the couch and stood. "As a matter of fact, I do."

Amy stepped outside of her comfort zone and walked toward the man who was drinking up every inch of her with his eyes. She definitely had to do this more often. She had a feeling it would be a rewarding night, and she wasn't going to waste another minute.

CHAPTER SEVENTEEN

Early the next morning, Amy shot up to a seated position in bed, startled from the loud knock on the guesthouse door. "Does anybody ever sleep around here?"

She wiped her eyes and glanced at the hunky man sleeping next to her, relieved that last night wasn't a dream.

More like a fantasy.

"Luke?" Grandpa Leo called from outside after another knock. "You up?"

Amy nudged Luke on the shoulder. "Hey, cowboy."

Luke rolled over and faced Amy. "General Maximus." He grinned and pulled her back down into his arms, holding her close.

She could spoon with him for hours, but now wasn't the best time. "General Maximus, we have invaders outside. Grandpa Leo and Grams. We should answer the door."

"They have a key. They'll be in shortly."

She settled back into his arms. "You're getting to know my family pretty well."

"General Maximus knows all."

"Maybe they went for a walk," Grams said from outside. "Check the door."

The handle jiggled.

"Nope," Grandpa Leo said. "Locked again. And why do you always assume people are out walking if they're not home?"

"Walking is healthy, and what else are they going to be doing? Come on—use the key."

Amy could hear jingling keys. The door flew open.

"Oh!" Grandpa Leo said. "Sorry about that. Didn't think you were here."

"Where else would they be?" Grams asked.

"Walking, according to you."

Amy sat up, holding the bed sheet close to her body, and hoping her grandparents wouldn't notice she was going to die from embarrassment. "Happy birthday, Grandpa."

Luke sat up like it was completely normal for grandparents to barge in on you when you're half-naked in bed. "Happy birthday."

"Thank you, thank you," Grandpa Leo said. "Ninety is a good number."

"And is this our ninety-minute warning about breakfast again?" Amy said.

"No, no. Nothing like that. We wanted to let you know Nathan is back."

"What?" Amy yelled.

Grams smacked Grandpa Leo on the arm. "Don't do that to the poor girl. Look at her. She turned whiter than rice."

Grandpa Leo frowned. "Sorry, sweetie pie. Bad joke. Nathan isn't here."

Grams crossed her arms and huffed. "Good luck with your birthday request now."

"What request?" Amy asked.

"I bought spareribs for Grandpa's birthday dinner. I was going to roast them in the oven, like I normally do, but the birthday boy was hoping Luke would smoke them on the grill."

"You mentioned Memphis-style was your specialty," Grandpa Leo said.

"It is, and it would be a pleasure," Luke said. "It'll take me five to six hours to smoke them."

"Wonderful!" Grandpa Leo said, lighting up. "How can we help?"

"I'll need some wood."

"We've got plenty of wood. Oak and hickory. I think we even have cherry."

"Oak and cherry are perfect."

"Amy can show you where it is. And thank you. This will be a special birthday meal."

And just like that Luke was doing something else for the family. The man was amazing on so many levels. Amy had told him he would fit right in since everything her family did revolved around food, and she was right. Luke had even offered to help her brainstorm ideas for additional income streams for the family business.

After breakfast, Amy took Luke out to show him the rest of the property. They walked hand-in-hand through the apple orchard. She pointed to the place where they kept the wood but then kept walking, enjoying the sights and sounds and smells of nature.

She sighed, realizing she missed it more than she had thought.

"This place is amazing," Luke said, letting go of her hand and doing a three-sixty. "I had no idea the property was so huge." He pointed to the hill in the distance. "Is that hill over there a part of your property, too?"

"All the way to the top."

He nodded, deep in thought. "You get snow here, right?"

"Sure do. Not a lot, but we get it. Enough snow to ride a saucer down that hill. I used to do it when I was a kid."

Amy's dad drove toward them in the UTV. Amy hadn't seen him all morning and was still waiting for that apology he had promised last night. It looked like he would keep his word.

Greg got out of the vehicle and approached them. "Good morning." His energy was low, and he avoided eye contact.

"Good morning," Luke and Amy said together.

Greg rubbed the back of his neck and cleared his throat, looking Luke in the eyes. "Look . . . I'm going to cut to the chase. I'm here to offer you an apology. I made a big mistake and I acted like an idiot more than a few times. I won't give you a bunch of excuses for my behavior. I want to say I'm sorry and I hope you can forgive me." He extended his hand.

Luke shook Greg's hand with a wide smile. "Apology accepted."

Crazy as it sounded, Amy got a little misty-eyed over that little exchange. This was feeling real. Like Luke was her fiancé. She glanced down at the ring on her finger, wondering what it would be like if they were really engaged. How was that possible to have such thoughts when they had only met last week?

"Good. Thank you. Besides, you're family now." Greg winked and squeezed Luke's shoulder. "What are you two doing all the way out here?"

"Brainstorming," Amy said. "You said you wanted to find more ways to generate money, and Luke offered to help."

Greg turned to Luke, his eyes widening. "I appreciate that. Have you come up with anything yet? The only thing I know is apples."

Luke pointed back toward the hill. "Well . . . I think you may have an opportunity right up there."

Greg squinted, following the direction of Luke's finger. "Yeah? I thought most of that hill was unusable. What do you have in mind?"

"Saucer and sled rentals in the winter. It would be a short season, since you don't get a lot of snow, but it's something."

Greg nodded. "It certainly is. What else?"

Luke pointed to the large open area off to the right. "You can do pony rides for kids there."

Amy and Greg both stared at him.

"What?" Luke said.

"How do you come up with this stuff?" Amy asked.

Luke chuckled. "I've had lots of coffee this morning and my brain likes caffeine." He spun back around and gestured back at the apple orchard. "And have you thought about planting more apple trees? You have so much land you're not using. You could have a U-Pick orchard and charge people to come pick their own apples and take them home. You can even make it a fun family event—picnic tables, hot dogs and burgers, that kind of thing. Something to think about."

"Definitely," Greg said, his energy picking up. "There are a couple of U-Pick apple farms in the area and they charge twenty bucks a bag for people to come pick organic apples. I don't see why we couldn't do the same."

"Or a pumpkin patch. Heck, that's a lot easier, I would imagine. Plant in May or June and have the pumpkins ready by late September. Add some face painting and jumpy houses for the kids and you've got another fun event for the family every year. I hear pumpkin patches make a lot of money."

"I like that idea," Amy said.

"I'll see what else I can come up with later," Luke said. "I should gather the wood for the smoker and prep the spareribs."

"You bet. Thanks again." Greg hopped in the UTV and drove back toward the main house.

Amy turned to Luke, running her hands up his chest. "You were right. General Maximus knows all."

"I know I want to kiss you." Luke leaned down and kissed Amy.

Amy pulled away from the kiss. "Okay—we'd better get to work."

Luke arched an eyebrow. "We?"

"I need to bake a practice version of the pie for tomorrow's contest."

"Oh. I didn't know you were going to enter."

"Hadn't planned on it but being back here in Julian kind of got me in the mood. It would be good for the family business, too. The exposure, you know. Plus, the proceeds from the entry fees and sales of the remaining slices all go to charity."

"I like that."

Amy playfully poked Luke in the chest. "And since *you* are a pie fanatic, you can be my official taste-tester. I should have it finished around lunchtime."

Luke threw his palms up to surrender. "You don't have to twist my arm. You can count on me for pie tasting and whatever else your heart desires."

Amy's heart had many desires for Luke, but she would have to take a raincheck on that. She needed to get her butt to the kitchen and focus on making that pie.

She was motivated to win that contest.

She had to win.

For the sake of the family farm.

CHAPTER EIGHTEEN

Amy studied the pie that sat on the cooler on top of the kitchen counter. She'd met judges who had docked points based on first impressions. The appearance was as important as the taste. She was sure she didn't have to worry about that. This had to be one of the best pies she'd ever made, from a visual standpoint. The color was even. The diamond pattern on the top crust was perfect. The rim crust was golden brown and flaky. She'd even brushed the crust with an egg wash and had sprinkled it with sparkly coarse sugar to give it some extra eye appeal.

"Looks like you haven't lost your touch," Grams said, wiping her hands. She had finished preparing the macaroni salad that would go with the smoked spareribs for Grandpa Leo's birthday dinner.

"The day I lose my touch is the day I quit my job."

"I doubt that will ever happen. Speaking of work . . . are you happy there at the hotel?"

Happy? Amy wouldn't say that. It was a job, that was

about it. The hotel was a great place to work and they treated their employees well, but she wasn't doing what she wanted to do. What she had wanted to do when she had graduated from culinary school so many years ago. She wanted to have her own business. She wanted to have more creative control.

"You didn't answer my question," Grams said.

She turned to Grams and forced a smile. "Sorry. My job is okay . . . I guess."

"Sounds like a ringing endorsement. Sign me up."

"I know, I know."

"Looks like someone needs to make a change. Follow your dreams. As your grandpa says, you only live once. You need to get back to your roots. Move back here."

"Did Dad tell you to say that?"

"No, but he could use your help with the company. He's not getting any younger, you know."

It was tempting. Being back these few days had made her realize that maybe she was living in the wrong place. She couldn't remember the last time she had felt relaxed and alive at the same time. The presence of a certain gladiator may have something to do with that.

Grams covered the macaroni salad with plastic wrap and slid it onto the bottom shelf of the fridge, then pulled out the mustard and mayo for the sandwiches they would have for lunch. "Thinking of your fiancé?"

"What?"

Grams pointed to Amy's face. "You were smiling. Looks like you had a man on your mind."

She nodded. "He's an amazing man. A smart one, too."

"*That* he is. Smart as a whip."

"He knows a lot about pies, too. He used to bake them

with his grandmother, like me." She took a few steps toward Grams and kissed her on the cheek.

"Is there anything that man doesn't do?"

Amy shook her head. "Not that I know of."

"Well good thing you're marrying him. He's a keeper." Grams scratched the side of her face. "Bread! Bread would be good." She disappeared inside the walk-in pantry.

"Where is everybody?" Amy asked. "Usually one of the guys is complaining by now that they're starving, but this place is deserted."

Grams came out of the pantry with a loaf of bread and set it on the counter next to the mayo and mustard. "Your dad, Gramps, and Ruben all went over to one of the U-Pick farms to spy on them. Jennie is horseback riding with some new guy she met, but says she's already fallen in love with. He'll be here for dinner."

"No wonder she disappeared! What about Aunt Barbara?"

"She's around here somewhere. Last I saw her she was laying out in the sun, testing some new natural sunblock oil she says has an SPF of a thousand."

Amy laughed. "Remind me to stay away from that oil."

Luke came in from the back patio. "Man, I'm starving."

Amy turned to Grams. "What did I tell you?"

He kissed Amy on the cheek and washed his hands in the sink. "What did you tell Grams?"

"Nothing important. Grab a seat."

He sat down and placed his hat on the empty chair next to him. "Did I mention I'm starving?"

Amy laughed. "You did. We're having sandwiches for lunch. Ham, salami, or bologna?"

"Ham, please. I have about twenty minutes before I need to get back and check on the spareribs."

"Sounds good," Amy said, looking forward to trying his barbecue for the first time.

After they finished their sandwiches, Amy grabbed Luke's plate and stuck it in the sink, then placed the pie in the center of the table. "Dessert! This is what I want to enter in the contest tomorrow."

Luke stared at it. "Wow. That looks amazing."

"Hopefully, it tastes even better." Amy sliced a piece for Luke and stuck it on a small dessert plate for him. Then she cut a slice for Grams and herself. She sat back down between Grams and Luke and pointed to his plate. "You first."

Luke grinned. "Don't mind if I do." He took a bite and chewed, nodding his head.

She leaned in to get a look at his eyes. "Well? Be honest."

He took another bite. "Mmm. Very good."

Grams took a bite. "He's right. Flaky. Moist. Tasty. Very good."

That's what she wanted to hear. She felt the same way but wanted to be sure.

Amy stared at the pie, proud of it. "How does it compare to the pies you sampled last night at the restaurant? That's important because I will most likely be competing against them again."

Luke thought about it for a moment. "It's at the same level as the other pies, for sure."

"Great!" Amy said, taking a bite of her own slice.

"Or . . . not so great."

Amy put down her fork and glanced at Luke. "Why not?"

"Well, how is your pie going to stand out if it's identical to the three pies from last night?"

Amy blinked twice.

She hadn't thought about it from that perspective.

Luke picked at the pie with his fork. "You wanted me to be honest."

"Of course."

"I think it needs a little something to take it to the next level—that's all. I think I even know what it is."

"Thanks, but that's not necessary."

This exact pie won the competition three years ago, and now Luke was telling her she needed to improve her award-winning pie? No way. Even if it needed a tweak, which it didn't, there wasn't time the day before the contest. She wasn't willing to take a chance, either.

Amy sighed. "If it's as good as the others, it will all come down to the judges. And the judges loved the last pie I made. Enough to give it first place, remember?"

Luke reached over and placed his hand on top of her hand, caressing it. "Fair enough. You have my vote." He winked at her and kissed her on the cheek.

"Amy tells me you used to bake pies with your grandmother," Grams said.

Luke smiled. "I did. I have great memories being with her in the kitchen, being covered in flour. She taught me a lot. My grandpa, too."

"That's sweet. What was your favorite pie?"

"It was called the *Double, Double, Double.*" He laughed. "My grandma let me name it when I was a kid obviously, but I kept the name over the years because it reminded me of her."

"What was in it?"

"Boysenberry and apple with double crust, double crumb, double dutch, and lots of butter."

"That sounds wonderful. Do you still have the recipe?'

Luke tapped on his temple with his index finger. "Right inside here. I've got it memorized. I'm guessing we made it a hundred times." He chuckled. "Best pie in the world."

"Oh . . ." Amy crossed her arms. "Better than mine?"

Luke chuckled. "Well . . . I may be a little biased."

"You should enter that pie in the contest," Grams said

He waved her off. "No, no, no. That's not going to happen."

"Why not? It's for charity. Plus, you said it was the best pie in the world. What have you got to lose?"

"My fiancée?"

"Nonsense. It would be fun if you and Amy were competing against each other."

Amy would have to disagree.

She'd gotten the shock of her life at the Double Deuce when Luke beat her at bull-riding. She had underestimated him, no doubt. She was done competing against him.

Not fun at all.

Anyway, it didn't matter.

Bull-riding was much different from baking pies.

Plus, she was a professional!

Luke glanced over at Amy, looking a little unsure and sheepish.

"Hey, don't look at me," she said. "You're a big boy. You can do whatever you want."

"There you go," Grams said, giving Luke the thumbs-up. "You have spousal approval. Enter the contest."

"I don't know . . ." He glanced at Amy again.

"If you want to enter the pie contest, go ahead," Amy said. "I dare you."

Amy had no idea why she dared him.

Her pride was controlling her mouth.

The problem was she'd never met a man who had backed down from a dare. Ever.

Amy and Luke sat there, staring at each other, neither one blinking.

It was like they were two gunslingers in a stand-off in in the middle of the deserted street in a tumbleweed town.

"Take back the dare," Luke said, looking amused.

Amy laughed. "No."

"Please."

She shook her head.

"Fine."

Amy blinked. "Fine *what*?"

"Fine. I'm entering the contest."

"Yes!" Grams said, pumping her fist in the air like a teenager.

Amy wasn't feeling Grams' enthusiasm at all.

Maybe it was that look on Luke's face.

The man was out of his league when it came to making pies, so how could he be so cool and confident? And how could Amy admire that and hate it at the same time?

Grams' chanting wasn't making Amy feel any better.

"Double, double, double spells trouble, trouble, trouble."

Amy clenched her jaw. "Stuff a sock in it, Grams."

Luke finished cutting up the smoked spareribs he'd prepared

for Grandpa Leo's birthday meal, then transferred them to the large platter on the center of the food table outside. They looked and smelled perfect. He couldn't wait for everyone to try them. Especially Grandpa Leo, since he was the guest of honor and the one who had requested them.

Amy inspected the spareribs on the platter.

"Hang on." Luke trimmed a little piece of meat off, sneaking it to her. "You didn't get this from me."

She laughed and popped the tender piece of meat into her mouth and chewed. "These are the same ribs you made on television to win the hundred thousand dollars?"

He nodded. "Same ones."

"Wow. Amazing."

"Thank you."

Amy held up a finger. "Although I think they need a little something to take them to the next level. I think I even know what it is."

He should have seen that coming.

Luke placed his hands on his hips. "I think I'm going to regret making that comment about your pie. Are you mad at me for entering the contest?"

She patted him on the chest. "Relax, cowboy. I'm just having fun with you. I'm not mad."

Luke wasn't so sure about that.

Amy flipped around and faced everyone on the patio. "It's suppertime. Get your grub on! Grandpa Leo and Grams are first to get food. The rest of you get in line after them to grab a plate."

They all formed a line behind Grandpa Leo and Grams, each person piling their plate high with ribs, macaroni salad, and cornbread. Luke and Amy grabbed some food and sat at the end of the large table next to Aunt Barbara.

Luke tried not to stare, but her face was tomato red and shiny.

"This is wonderful," Aunt Barbara said. "Thanks so much, Luke."

"It was my pleasure."

She picked up Luke's hand, inspecting it. "Oh dear, what happened?"

"Just a little burn from the smoker. All part of the job. It's fine."

"I will patch you up in a jiffy," she said, grabbing her bag and opening it up. She pulled out one of the bottles of oil and squirted some on her fingertips, gently massaging the burn on Luke's hand. "This is a wonderful blend of lavender, melaleuca, and peppermint. It's the same oil I have on my face at the moment. As you can tell, I spent a little too much time in the sun today and made the mistake of applying an oil I thought was SPF one thousand. Shoulda had my glasses on when I read the bottle because it was only SPF 10!" She gave him back his hand. "There you go."

"Thank you," Luke said, even though it was now burning like hell.

Grandpa Leo cleared his throat. "Dearly beloved, we are gathered here today to drink beer and eat a bunch of food."

"Don't talk too long or the food will get cold," Grams said.

"Okay, okay. I want to say thank you all for coming to my birthday. I'm so old I remember when the Dead Sea was just sick." Everyone laughed. "Anyway, a special thanks to Luke for smokin' up these fantastic ribs. And welcome to the family!" He held up his glass.

"Cheers!" everybody yelled together.

Grandpa Leo sat back down next to Grams and kissed her. She smiled and patted him on the hand.

That sure is sweet.

Luke loved how in love they were with each other, even after so many years. He nudged Amy's shoulder with his own shoulder. "How long have they been married?"

Amy nudged him back. "Grandpa Leo married her when he was twenty-five, so they'll be celebrating their sixty-fifth wedding anniversary on December twenty-third."

"Wow." He continued to watch them, in awe. "Sixty-five years married."

"Yup."

He turned to Amy and whispered. "Do you think our fake marriage can last that long?"

She thought about it for a moment. "I would be a hundred and ten."

"And?"

"And . . . I would be ancient or dead."

"Yeah," he said, reaching under the table and grabbing her hand. "But I bet you wouldn't look a day over a hundred." He squeezed her hand, leaned closer, and kissed her on the lips.

This was getting serious. He could feel it.

With every word, with every kiss, with every touch, he was falling more and more for Amy. She pulled away from the kiss and glanced up at him with that thousand-watt-smile, her eyes telling him she was feeling something, too.

Something special.

"All right you two," Amy's dad said. "Save that for later, would ya?"

"Yes, sir, Mr. Weaver."

"Please. Call me Greg." He winked and picked up one of his ribs, tearing into it and nodding his appreciation. "Good stuff."

That was a first. Who said people weren't able to change?

Luke glanced toward the other end of the table at Amy's niece. She was chatting with some man he hadn't seen before.

"Who's the new guy with Jennie?"

Amy shrugged. "I have no idea, but supposedly she is already in love with him, at least according to Grams."

"That's a different guy than the one she was with the day we arrived, right?"

"Yeah. That's why I'm very skeptical of her supposed feelings. It doesn't happen that fast."

No? Luke's feelings for Amy were growing at an alarming rate.

He picked up his piece of cornbread and inspected it. "This looks different than your average everyday cornbread. What's in it?"

"I'll tell you after you take a bite. Dip it in the barbecue sauce."

Luke dipped the cornbread in the barbecue sauce, then took a bite. His eyes grew wide, He glanced over at Amy and then dipped more into the sauce, taking another bite. Then he licked his fingers.

"I guess that means you like it," Amy said.

"Yes. Please tell me what I'm eating." He took another bite and couldn't stop himself from moaning. He took the last bite and shook his head, still confused as ever.

Amy laughed. "Jalapeño-corn-beer-bread."

"Love it. Who made it?"

Amy smiled and waved her hand.

"No. You?"

Amy lost her smile and held up her fist. "Don't say it."

"What? I wasn't going to say anything!"

After they finished their meals, Luke whispered in Amy's ear, "I need to talk with you. It'll be too obvious if we both leave together. I'm going to get up and walk away. In two minutes, you do the same and meet me over by the barn."

She leaned closer to his ear. "Now? What is it?"

"I'll tell you when you meet me at the barn."

"Luke," she said, trying to grab his hand but not being able to hang on.

"Don't you go too far," Grams said. "We're bringing out the birthday cake soon."

"Sounds good," Luke said. "I'll be right back." He winked at Amy and walked around the corner toward the barn.

A few minutes later, Amy hurried in his direction. "Okay, what couldn't wait?"

"This," Luke said, taking Amy in his arms and kissing her. "Sorry—I had to do that."

"I'm . . . uh . . . okay."

Luke chuckled. "I know we should get back for the cake, but there's something I wanted to say."

"Okay . . ."

"I can see you're skeptical of people developing feelings quickly, but it's happening to me. Big time. I know it's crazy, but there were times yesterday and today when I forgot we were faking it."

Amy nodded. "Me, too."

"This deal was only supposed to be for the week, but I don't want it to end. I want to keep seeing you when we get back to San Diego."

"I'd like that very much, too."

"Good. Come here." He pulled her closer and kissed her again. After a couple of minutes, he realized they were still by the barn, and there was a cake and many people waiting for them. That kiss was better than the best cake or pie in the world, but he had to break it off. "Okay, your kiss distracted me, and I forgot what I was going to say. Oh, that's right. What do we tell your family about us and our engagement? I'm becoming attached to your grandparents and don't want to hurt them."

"I know, I know. I saw none of this coming myself." Amy sighed. "Honestly—let's get through the next couple of days and I'll figure something out, something to tell them. The main thing is to stay the course and keep doing what we're doing. We don't want to slip up now."

"I agree."

"If worse comes to worst, we'll tell the family we have so much going on that we're putting the wedding on the back burner to concentrate on business, while I figure a way out of the financial issues my father has."

Luke and Amy returned to the party and were about to take their seats when Jennie and her mysterious new man approached.

"Hi, Auntie Amy." Jennie gave her a hug. "I haven't seen you in a while."

Amy crossed her arms. "*You* kind of disappeared. Still looking for that scrunchy?"

Jennie let out a nervous laugh. "I always seem to lose those little buggers." She gestured to the man. "This is my boyfriend Marcus."

"Boyfriend?" Amy said.

Jennie smiled. "That's right." She leaned closer to Amy. "I think he's *the one*."

That was fast.

Grams came out of the house with the birthday cake and placed it on the table in front of Grandpa Leo. "There we are. Uh-oh, where's the lighter?" She went back inside the house and came right back out with the lighter a few seconds later. "Here we go."

Grandpa Leo stared at all the candles on the top. "A blow-torch would be easier."

Grams laughed and lit the candles.

They all sang "Happy Birthday" to Grandpa Leo, and then Grams sliced up the cake and passed the slices around the table.

A few minutes later, Greg knelt down in between Amy and Luke's chairs. "Thanks again for taking the time to make the spareribs. They were the best I've ever had."

"My pleasure, Greg. Glad you enjoyed them."

Greg turned to his daughter. "All set for the pie contest tomorrow?"

"Yup," Amy said. "I'm setting the alarm for five to get an early start."

"That's my girl." He turned to Luke. "Grams said you were entering the contest, too."

"That's right."

Greg thought about it for a moment. "You ever baked a pie for a competition before?"

"No, I haven't."

"Baked professionally?"

"No, sir."

Greg laughed. "Okay, I get it. You're doing it for fun. Nothing wrong with that."

Luke opened his mouth and then closed it. No need to convince Amy's father he knew how to bake a pie. A damn good pie.

He wondered what Greg would think if he won the contest.

Only time would tell.

Luke wasn't a professional pie maker, but there was one thing for sure.

He always played to win.

CHAPTER NINETEEN

The woman waved to the crowd as she approached the micro-phone in the middle of the stage. "I hope you're all enjoying the Julian Country Fair!" She waited for the applause to die down. "And now we've come to my favorite part of the fair, the pie competition!" She gestured to the pie tables off to the side of the stage, each one with a number in front of it. "As you know, we normally judge the pies in top secrecy behind closed doors, but the response this year was so overwhelming we needed a larger space. Well, that and we are going to be on national television! Wave to the cameras!"

The audience stood and cheered, turning toward the many cameras and waving.

Amy stood from her chair in the front row, applauding, more concerned with where Luke was. He'd gone to get a beer, but he sure was taking his sweet time. Or maybe it only seemed like he was gone forever because Amy was nervous.

Nervous as hell.

It didn't make sense because she was sure her pie turned

out even better than the one she'd made yesterday. Better than the one that had won the contest three years ago. She'd gotten up at five in the morning and meticulously prepared the pie in the kitchen of the main house as if her life depended on it.

Maybe it did.

Luke prepared his mysterious "Double, Double, Double" pie in the guesthouse kitchen and continued to appear very confident about it. Amy had to admit his pie looked impressive, but that couldn't have been what was making her uptight. Maybe her nerves were there because she knew the family was counting on her to win.

Luke returned with the beer and they both sat.

"Finally!" Amy said.

"What?" Luke said, looking around. "Did I miss something?"

"No." She eyed the large beer cup in his hand. "Can I have a sip?"

"Of course." He handed her the beer.

Amy drank a few giant gulps without breathing, then handed the cup back to him.

Luke peeked inside the cup and chuckled. "I should have gotten you one."

"I told you, I didn't want one."

"Could've fooled me. You okay?"

"Fine." Amy pressed her palm down on the top of her leg to settle it when she realized it was bouncing up and down.

"Why is everyone cheering? Nothing is happening."

Amy pointed to the cameras. "To be on television, I guess."

He nodded. "Ahhhh."

The woman on stage raised her hand to silence the crowd.

"Let me recap the rules and then we'll get to the results of the pie contest." She glanced down at the notes on her clipboard. "Remember that all pies entered must be homemade. Every contestant had to submit their recipe with the exact list of ingredients of the pie they baked. At least one ingredient must be apples. The judges evaluated the pies based on overall appearance and presentation, taste and texture of the crust and the filling, and creativity. And let's hear it for our judges!"

The judges rose from their chairs at the back of the stage and waved to the audience.

The crowd cheered.

"I thought Grandpa Leo and Grams were going to be here," Luke said.

"They're over there by the side of the stage with my dad," Amy said, pointing.

"Okay, then . . . let's get to the winners!" the woman continued. One judge stood and walked over to the woman, handing her a slip of paper.

Luke leaned closer and kissed Amy on the lips. "Good luck."

"Thank you," she said, grabbing his beer and taking another chug.

The woman on stage cleared her throat. "Don't forget . . . slices of all the pies from the competition will go on sale after I announce the winners. All proceeds go to charity. I know I'll be trying a few, for sure. Okay, Honorable mention goes to . . ." She paused for the drumroll. "Marlene Jacoby for her cherry apple crumb! Please stand and take a bow, Marlene."

Marlene stood and waved to the crowd as they cheered and applauded. Then she blew a kiss to one of the television cameras and sat back down.

"And second place goes to . . ." She paused for another drumroll. "Amy Weaver from Pie in the Sky, for her classic apple pie!"

Amy felt ill.

It was difficult to breathe.

She could barely swallow.

I didn't win. I got second place.

She glanced at Luke.

He reached over and kissed her. "Congratulations. There were a lot of pies this year, so second place is a huge accomplishment."

A huge disappointment was more like it.

She glanced over at her dad standing by the side of the stage.

He shook his head and then massaged his temples.

This wasn't good.

Not good at all.

"Stand up, Amy!" the woman said.

Amy stood and used every ounce of energy she had to force a smile as she waved to the audience and the television cameras. Then she sat back down.

"Okay, the moment we've all been waiting for. This year's Julian Country Fair pie champion is . . . " She paused for the last drumroll. "Luke Jenkins for his Double, Double, Double pie!"

The audience cheered and applauded and whistled.

Amy could hear Grams' chant from yesterday echoing in her head.

Double, double, double spells trouble, trouble, trouble.

Grams had been right.

Luke won.

Amy should have been happy for him.

He was a good man and his pie impressed the judges.

But there was one other thing stuck in her head.

One thing that could haunt her for years to come.

If Luke hadn't entered the contest, Amy would've won again.

"Come on up to the stage, Luke!"

Amy turned to Luke, trying to appear sincere. "Congratulations."

Luke kissed her. "Thank you." He gestured to the stage. "I guess I should get up there."

"Yeah . . ."

He squeezed her hand and winked. "Be right back." He stood and tipped his hat to the audience and the cameras before heading up to the stage.

Amy watched in envy as the woman pinned the winner's ribbon on Luke's shirt and handed him the first prize check.

They posed for a few pictures before she gestured to him and said, "Once again, let's hear it for Luke Jenkins, our first-place winner!"

Amy walked to the stairs by the stage and waited for him, deep in thought.

She needed to feel happy for him, but all she could feel was heartbreak.

Luke waved one more time to the crowd, then came down the stairs from the stage. "I can't believe this. Can you?"

No. "You deserve it," Amy said.

A man with a *Press* lanyard around his neck approached Luke. "Excuse me, Mr. Jenkins. If you could please follow me to the media tent. They'd like to record your interview segment."

"Of course." Luke glanced over at Amy. "Sorry."

"Don't be," she said, almost relieved she could escape since she had no idea what to say to him at this point. "I understand. Go. I'll see you later."

"I have no idea how long this will be. Go have fun and enjoy the festival. I'll text you when I'm done. Oh, you should take this." Luke handed Amy his beer.

Have fun. Enjoy the festival.

Right. There was zero chance of that happening.

Amy slammed the rest of his beer, tossed the cup in the trash, and watched him walk away with the man toward the media tent.

I should've won. That should be me.

"We need to talk," Greg said.

Amy swung around, not in the mood to talk with anyone, especially her dad. "What?"

"Not here."

Amy sighed and followed her dad away from the throngs of people hanging around the stage.

He stopped near the exit of the pumpkin patch where Grandpa Leo and Grams were sitting on a bench underneath a tree.

"Congratulations, sweetie." Grandpa Leo stood and hugged Amy.

Grams gave Amy a sympathetic smile. "Second place is still amazing. Otherwise they wouldn't have the silver medal in the Olympics."

"Nobody remembers who wins the silver medals," Greg said. "Luke ruined everything."

Amy placed her hands on her hips. "No, he didn't."

"We had a plan. You were supposed to win. He had to

have known how much that win would mean to us. Why would he even enter the contest?"

Because I dared him.

"The future of our company was at stake," her dad continued. "He doesn't care about you or the family. He only cares about himself. What a selfish bastard."

"How dare you talk about Luke that way?" Amy said, feeling her pulse hammering in her temples. "He's the most decent man I have ever met."

Greg chuckled. "Right. Decent . . . Face the facts, your fiancé is a loser."

Amy took a step toward her dad, on the verge of exploding. "I'll tell you who the loser is. You! You know why? Because I had to hire Luke to pretend to be my fiancé because *you* wouldn't stop forcing Nathan on me. How pathetic is that?"

Greg just stared at Amy.

"Come again?" Grandpa Leo said.

"Huh?" Grams said.

Amy blinked twice.

Crap.

That's what happens when someone keeps pushing your buttons. Eventually, you can't control your emotions, or your mouth, and you say something that was supposed to stay inside your head. She should've walked away when he said he wanted to talk.

Amy could feel the intense stares of her dad, Grams, and Grandpa Leo, but she decided the best solution altogether was to avoid eye contact with them and pretend they weren't even there. She looked off into the distance toward the petting zoo, took a deep breath, and tried to regain her composure.

Breathe. Everything will be okay.

"Is this true?" her dad asked. "You and Luke are—"

"*Not* engaged." Amy glanced down at her hand on the verge of tears. She pulled and twisted and pulled, finally able to get the ring off her finger. She held it up. "*This* is Jennie's ring. I met Luke last week in a bar."

"I don't care where you met him," Grandpa Leo said. "I like the guy."

"Me too," Grams added. "You two are good together. I can't believe it wasn't real. That man loves you."

Amy wasn't sure what to believe anymore, but that was it.

Their charade was over.

What would happen between her and Luke now? She'd been living in a dreamworld to think someone so perfect could be interested in someone as imperfect as her.

"Luke is a fraud *and* a loser?" her dad said. "You know how to pick 'em."

This was the first time in Amy's life that she was tempted to kick her dad in the nuts, but she opted to turn her back on him instead. Then she sent a text to Luke saying she wasn't feeling well and was going home. He knew his way back, so no big deal.

She needed to get out of there.

She needed space to think.

She needed to figure out what she wanted to do with the rest of her life.

Luke stared at the text he had just received from Amy. He scratched his head, confused. She got sick? She didn't look sick ten minutes ago. Sure, she'd drank his beer pretty fast, but that couldn't have been it. Especially after seeing how she handled her tequila at the Double Deuce.

The thought of how they met made him smile.

He typed his reply to make sure she was okay and—

"Hold still," the makeup artist said.

"Sorry." Luke slipped the phone back in his pocket.

"A little more and you'll be good to go." The woman was applying something to his face so he wouldn't be shiny on camera for the interview.

Luke was sure Amy's sickness wasn't physical at all. She said she felt bad, not sick. There was no doubt she felt bad about getting second place in the contest. She'd looked even worse after Luke was announced the first-place winner. She tried to play it off as if she were happy for him, but he wasn't a fool. Amy's usual thousand-watt-smile hadn't had enough energy to power up a bathroom nightlight. It was obviously a mistake to enter the contest, even if she had dared him.

"They're ready for Mr. Jenkins," a producer said.

The makeup artist smiled. "All done."

Luke followed the producer to another section of the giant tent where there were bright lights and three cameras set up for the interview. He wasn't nervous at all. He'd been through this before when he was on *Barbecue Pitmasters* and he enjoyed it.

The interview didn't last too long and went off without a hitch. The producer thanked Luke and let him know the segment would air tomorrow on television.

Ten minutes later, Luke drove up the long driveway to Amy's family's farmhouse, admiring the apple trees on both sides of the driveway. He loved Julian and could even picture himself living the small town life. Speaking of which, he needed to remember to talk with Emilio before he headed back to San Diego. The conversation they'd had about becoming a partner at Main Street Grub & Pub piqued Luke's interest. It would be an amazing opportunity.

Luke parked his truck by the left side of the barn and walked straight to the guesthouse to see how Amy was doing. If she was still feeling bad he would pamper her with a foot massage and whatever else he could think of to make her feel better. His feelings for her were too strong to let the pie contest come between them.

Luke swung the door open and froze.

Amy's dad was standing there, his arms crossed, not looking happy at all.

"Hey, Greg."

"It's Mr. Weaver to you."

Here we go again. What did I do this time?

"Mr. Weaver . . . have you seen Amy?"

"I have. And she doesn't want to see you anymore."

"What are you talking about?"

"She's gone."

"What?"

Greg gestured around the room. "Look for yourself."

Luke glanced around the room, confused. Was Amy really gone? He didn't see any of her belongings anywhere. He slid the closet door open. Her suitcase and clothes on her side of the closet were gone. He stuck his head in the bathroom and clicked on the light. The beauty products that were on the counter were gone, too.

Luke rubbed the back of his neck. "I don't get it. What's going on here?"

"Do I need to spell it out for you, Luke? Or should I call you Mr. Fake Fiancé?"

This wasn't good.

Amy said to stick to the plan. Why would she tell her dad about it? Was she that upset about not winning the pie contest? Had she given up on everything?

Luke swallowed hard. "Where is she? Why doesn't she want to see me?"

"Because you ruined her life—that's why. My life, too."

"And how did I do that?"

Greg crossed his arms. "Do you realize what we had riding on this contest?"

"I—"

"Any chance of her career advancing was flushed down the toilet when she was beaten by you. An amateur. She's probably already the laughingstock of the pie industry. And any chance of our company surviving was also tossed in the shitter because of you. It may be all fun and games to you, but this is our livelihood."

The man was obviously exaggerating. If this contest was important to her career and the company, why hadn't anyone said anything? And why had Amy dared him to enter? None of this made sense.

"You ruined everything and it's time for you to leave." Greg pointed to the white envelope sitting on the bed. "That's for you, from Amy. Pack up and get your things out of my house, now. I never want to see you around here again." He walked out, but not before slamming the door.

Luke stood there in disbelief.

What just happened?

This was all because of a pie contest?

He glanced over at the envelope on the bed. Curious, he walked over and picked it up. His name was written on the outside. He opened it and pulled out a stack of hundred-dollar bills. Twelve, to be exact. It was the money Amy had agreed to pay him for being her fake fiancé. He thought he still had a couple of days left on the job, but obviously she had decided he wasn't needed anymore. He looked back inside the envelope. There was a note from Amy.

Luke,

Thank you.

Amy

That was it? He turned the note over to see if she had written something else on the other side, but it was blank. How could that be? Had she forgotten about their amazing week together? The night they shared and the things they said to each other. Was it all a game to her, to get rid of Nathan? Was it business and nothing more?

No. She felt something—he knew she did.

It wasn't enough.

Her dad was a complete jackass, but he was right about something.

Amy was done with him.

She'd made her decision and disappeared.

Luke sat down on the bed, his gut churning. Last night he had pictured spending the rest of his life with Amy. Now, he had to imagine a life without her.

Quit feeling sorry for yourself. You were hired to do a job, and you did it to the best of your ability. You're not wanted anymore, so move on.

It wasn't going to be easy. He grabbed his suitcase from the closet and set it on a chair, opening it. It didn't take long before he was packed and out the door.

Amy may not want to see Luke, but he sure as hell was going to say goodbye to Grams and Grandpa Leo. He approached the house and—

"Where do you think you're going?" Greg asked, standing on the front porch and blocking the front door.

"I want to say goodbye to Grams and Grandpa Leo."

"They're not here."

Luke eyed the house, not sure he believed Greg, but there was nothing he could do about it. It wasn't Luke's property. He didn't make the rules.

"Please tell them I said goodbye," Luke said.

Greg glared at Luke. "Whatever you say."

Luke shook his head and walked away, knowing Greg wasn't going to tell them a thing. He threw his suitcase in the extended cab of his truck and closed the door, ready to get out of there. He had to make one pit stop before he headed back to San Diego.

A few minutes later, Luke pulled his truck up in front of

Main Street Grub & Pub in downtown Julian. He had promised Emilio he would talk with him before he left town and he was a man of his word.

Luke stared at the front door of Emilio's place, not ready to go in yet because his thoughts wandered back to Amy and their date there. Their time together. How she felt in his arms. Their intimate conversations. The feelings he had for her.

How could Amy not know how much he cared for her? That he would give her the world?

He didn't need to worry about that.

Soon she would find out for herself.

CHAPTER TWENTY

The next morning, Amy shot up to a seated position in bed, startled from her ringing cellphone on the bedside table. She rubbed her eyes and looked over at the time on the alarm clock. It wasn't even seven o'clock yet. Not good since it had taken her forever to fall asleep.

Does anyone value sleep anymore?

Amy had planned on sleeping in until at least ten to make sure there was no chance of seeing any part of *Good Morning America* since Luke's interview segment from the pie contest was airing today. Then she would bake most of the day and give it away.

Her plan wasn't off to a good start.

She glanced at the caller ID on the phone. It was Grams, so she picked up.

"Grams? Is everything okay?"

"Can you come downstairs?" Grams said.

"Now?"

"Yes. Now."

Last night, Amy had slept in her childhood bedroom upstairs in the main house because the guesthouse reminded her too much of Luke. Grams didn't like to use the stairs, so Amy told her to call if she needed anything. She actually hadn't expected a call so early. This had better be good because it was almost impossible for Amy to fall back asleep once she was already awake.

"Are you there?" Grams asked.

"I'm here. Is everything okay? Is it Grandpa?"

"No—I need something from the guesthouse. Can you get it for me?"

Amy glanced at the clock again. "Now?"

Grams sighed. "Fine. Don't worry about it. I'll ask my other granddaughter. Oh wait—I don't have another granddaughter. Hmmm. What a predicament I seem to be in."

"Not funny."

"I would do it myself, but I'm preparing a mushroom and egg casserole for breakfast. And it looks like I'll have to eat this whole darn thing all by myself since you have no plans on coming downstairs."

"I'll be right there."

Amy could always be bribed with food. Especially when it was her favorite breakfast. She used the bathroom, changed clothes, and headed downstairs.

The smell coming from the kitchen was divine.

Amy kissed Grams on the cheek, then peeked through the window of the oven at the mushroom and egg casserole. "That looks amazing, but I know what you're up to. You wanted to get me down here to watch *Good Morning America* with you. Not going to happen."

Grams wiped her hands on the kitchen towel and tossed it on the counter. "Do you think I would do such a thing?"

"Yes." She pointed to the television that was on but muted. "I told you last night I can't see Luke on television or in person for a while. It would be too painful and I'm still embarrassed and sensitive about the whole thing."

"And I told you last night—I don't believe it's over between you two, either. It's a bump in the road, that's all."

"A bump? More like Mount Whitney." Amy blew out a frustrated breath. "Besides, he took the money and ran. I'm willing to bet there are skid marks in the driveway. Plus, the man didn't even have the decency to say goodbye. What does that say about him? It says he doesn't care, or he's mad at me." Amy was on the verge of crying but was trying to hold it together. "I appreciate you making my favorite breakfast and I know I will enjoy it like I always do, but I'm out of here when *Good Morning America* comes on. I want to be clear on that."

Grams nodded and poured herself a cup of coffee. "Fine, but I still need you to go to the guesthouse. Can you at least do that for me?"

"*That* I can do," Amy said, pouring herself a cup of coffee and adding cream and sugar. "What do you need?"

"The bedsheets and the towels from the bathroom."

Amy raised an eyebrow. "You woke me up for that?"

"It's important. I need to do a load of laundry and I don't want to burn your casserole."

Amy took a sip of her coffee and then set it on the kitchen table to finish later. On the walk to the guest house, she stopped and took in a deep breath. It always smelled so fresh and clean in Julian. After she entered the guesthouse, she closed the door behind her and leaned against the back of the door. She inhaled and could still smell Luke in the room even though he was long gone. How could the memory of him be so painful? She glanced over at the king-size bed.

What a night that was.

It would take a while to get Luke out of her system, there was no doubt about that, but being in the guesthouse wasn't making it any easier. She needed to get the bedsheets and towels and get out of there.

Amy headed to the bathroom for the towels and froze when she saw the envelope she had left for Luke. It was sitting on top of the desk next to a yellow piece of paper. Had he taken the money and left the empty envelope? Was there a note for her inside?

She opened the envelope and looked inside.

It was Luke's money, the twelve hundred dollars.

Amy stared at the cash and flipped through the bills.

Why it was still there made no sense.

Her dad had told her that Luke smiled when he had counted the money and then stuffed the cash in his pocket before walking out the door with his suitcase.

She set the envelope back on the desk and unfolded the yellow piece of paper next to it.

It was Luke's recipe for his *Double, Double, Double* pie handwritten on the back of a flyer for the Julian Old Fashioned Country Fair.

Why would he write the recipe on a piece of paper when he said he had it memorized? At the bottom he had also written, "Property of Amy Weaver."

Maybe it was the lack of caffeine in her system, but she was having a hard time understanding what was going on and why he had written that at the bottom. It wasn't her recipe.

She folded the recipe, grabbed the envelope of money, and walked back to the main house.

"Good morning, sweetie pie," Grandpa Leo said.

Aunt Barbara came in from the patio. "Good morning, everyone."

"Good morning," Amy said to them both. She kissed her grandpa on the cheek and took a seat at the kitchen table.

Grams placed a plate of the egg casserole in front of Amy. "There you go."

"Thank you," Amy said.

"You're welcome," Grams said, cutting up another piece of the casserole. "Did you put the bedsheets and towels by the washing machine?"

"Sorry—I need to go back and get them. I forgot when I got distracted by this." She held up the envelope and the recipe to show her grandmother.

"What is it?"

"The money I paid Luke and the recipe for his pie."

Grams chanted, "Double, double, double, spells trouble, trouble—"

"Grams."

"You have to admit it's kind of catchy."

"Not really," Grandpa Leo said.

Amy glanced down at the envelope and recipe in her hand. "Why would Luke leave this behind?"

"Because he wanted you to have it," Grams said.

"It doesn't make any sense. Dad said Luke took the money and left with a smile on his face. Like that was all he cared about. If that's the case, how did the money end up back in the room?"

Grams scooped up some egg casserole, put it on another

plate, and set it down in front of Grandpa Leo at the table. "Look . . . he's my son and I love him because I have no other choice, but that doesn't mean I believe everything that comes out of his mouth or approve of his actions."

Amy stared at Grams. "He lied?"

Grams pointed to Greg who entered the kitchen. "Why don't you ask your dad?"

Greg poured himself a cup of coffee. "Good morning. Smells good." He sat at the table and took a sip of his coffee. "What did you want to ask me?"

Amy was about to take a bite but set her fork back down on the table. "Did you lie when you said you saw Luke leave with the money?"

Greg hesitated. "Of course not."

"Then why was the money still in the guesthouse?"

"He left without the money?"

Amy nodded and shook the envelope. "All of it."

Greg stared at the envelope. "Oh." He cleared his throat. "Well, I didn't actually *see* him leave with it. He had it in his hand and he was getting ready to leave. I assumed he would leave with it." He pointed to the yellow piece of paper. "What's that?"

"The recipe for his pie that won the contest. He also left it."

Greg held out his hand. "Let me see that."

"No."

"Pardon me?"

"I said no. I don't trust you."

Greg glared at Amy. "You don't trust your own father?"

"That's right, I don't."

"I don't, either," Grandpa Leo said.

"Me neither," Grams said.

Greg blinked. "Have you all lost your minds?"

"Ha!" Amy said, laughing. "We should ask you that. You have issues, Dad."

"Issues . . ." He huffed and took a bite of his casserole. "I don't have issues."

"Denial, too. Ever since Mom died you haven't been the same. I understand it's been hard on you, but you have been taking it out on everybody else. It pains me to say you're not a nice person at all."

"I can't believe—"

"I haven't finished yet," Amy said. "You're quick to judge people and you're rude. I still can't believe the way you treated Luke. And while we're at it, you're letting the company go to shit, too. Maybe this is a good time for an intervention."

Grandpa Leo nodded. "Good idea."

"*Great* idea," Grams said. "But let's eat before it gets cold."

Amy didn't have a problem with that.

Grams pointed to the television. "Turn that up."

"You got it, my love." Grandpa Leo grabbed the remote and turned up the volume.

"No TV," Amy said, turning around and freezing when she saw Luke on *Good Morning America*. He looked amazing.

"Turn the channel, please," her dad said.

"No," Amy said.

It was too late. Now that she'd seen Luke, she couldn't look away. She couldn't move a muscle.

The man was kryptonite.

"Volume, please," Grams said.

Grandpa Leo clicked the volume button a few times. "At your service."

The news reporter smiled and gestured to Luke. "We're here at the Julian Country Fair with this year's winner of the annual pie competition, Luke Jenkins. Welcome to the show, Luke."

"It's a pleasure to be here," Luke said, appearing calm for being on national television.

"I have to say, what you've accomplished today is quite impressive. The field in the competition was stacked with some heavy hitters from the pie industry, some contestants with over twenty years of baking experience. You came into your first baking competition with plenty of experience as a barbecue pitmaster, but none as a baker in a professional capacity. You were an unknown and knocked it out of the park with your *Double, Double, Double* pie. Tell us about the winning pie and the inspiration behind it."

"I'd be happy to," Luke said. "The *Double, Double, Double* is a boysenberry and apple pie with double crust, double crumb, and double dutch. The extra butter makes it pop when you take the first bite. Well, every bite." He laughed.

"He's got a cute laugh," Grams said.

"Sure does," Aunt Barbara added.

"Shhh!" Amy said, leaning forward in her chair.

"As for the inspiration behind it," Luke said. "My grandma taught me how to make this pie when I was a kid. She's gone now, but it always reminds me of her. Now, if you want to talk about the inspiration for entering the contest, that would have to go to Amy Weaver."

Grandpa Leo pointed to the TV. "He mentioned you, sweetie pie!"

"I told you that man loves you," Grams said.

"Does he have makeup on?" Aunt Barbara said.

Greg pointed to the TV. "This is ridiculous. That man fooled us all. Please turn that off."

"No," Amy, Grandpa Leo, Grams, and Aunt Barbara all said together.

The news reporter looked surprised. "You're talking about *the* Amy Weaver? The second-place winner in the contest?"

Luke nodded. "The one and only. She's one of the sweetest, kindest, and most talented women I've ever met. I'm surprised she didn't win."

"Sounds like Amy Weaver has a secret admirer."

Luke grinned. "Oh, it's no secret at all."

"I told you that man's a keeper," Grams said. "But do you listen? Nooooooo."

Amy felt her face heat up.

She twisted back around toward the table, grabbed her orange juice, and took a big swig.

"Somebody is blushing," Grams said.

Amy took another big sip. "Stuff a sock in it, Grams."

"This was a big win and it must thrill you," the news anchor said. "What can we expect from you next?"

"Well, I'm excited about the future. I've always wanted to have my own restaurant and I'm going to be talking to someone about partnering up to open one of the largest barbecue restaurants and wedding venues on the West Coast."

"That sounds exciting. One more thing before we go . . . are people going to be able to try this award-winning pie soon? I know I want to."

Luke chuckled. "I'll save you a piece. And yes, people all across the country will be able to try the pie very soon. I've already received a couple of voicemail messages in the last few minutes about distribution. I can tell you this much, no matter what I decide, the *Double, Double, Double* will be available exclusively through Pie in the Sky in Julian, California. Check their website for updates."

"Well, it sounds like you've got a big hit on your hands and I'm sure many of our viewers are anxious to try it. Thanks for stopping by."

"My pleasure."

Amy was speechless.

"Woohoo!" Grams yelled.

Grandpa Leo clicked off the TV, set the remote down, and turned toward Amy's dad. "What do you think of Luke now? I liked him from day one. That is one generous man."

Greg stared off into the distance.

"I think it's time I took over the company," Amy blurted out.

"What?" Amy's dad said, coming out of his coma and almost falling out of his chair. "Where is this coming from?"

Grams lit up and placed a hand on her chest. "That is a *wonderful* idea."

"I can't think of a better person suited for the job," Aunt Barbara said.

"I agree!" Grandpa Leo said. "All in favor?"

Amy, Grandpa Leo, Grams, and Aunt Barbara all raised their hands.

"Sold! Amy is the new CEO of Pie in the Sky!"

Amy, Grandpa Leo, Grams, and Aunt Barbara all cheered and hugged.

"You can't be serious," Greg said.

"Very," Amy said, so full of life and confidence she wanted to explode. "You told me you don't have the energy anymore. You're stressed out and you're unhappy. I've been unhappy at my job too, because I belong here. It took me a while to realize that. It's also clear *you* need to retire."

"Another wonderful idea!" Grams said. "You said you always wanted to take a trip around the world. Well, now's the time. Chop, chop!"

Amy jumped up from her chair. "Okay, gotta go. I have a lot to do." She leaned over the table and took a few quick bites of the casserole, then ran around the table kissing everyone.

Greg sat there, looking like he'd just been hit in the head with a two-by-four.

"Oh, no!" Amy stopped, realizing she forgot something very important. "I don't have a car! Luke drove us here."

"Take mine," Grandpa Leo said.

Amy couldn't ever remember a time when someone other than Grandpa Leo had driven that car. It was the coolest car in the world. A cherry-red, 1958 Plymouth Belvedere Sport Coupe in mint condition. He kept it covered in the garage and only took it out on Sundays.

Now he was going to let her use it? Just like that?

"Why are you looking at me that way?" Grandpa Leo asked.

"You're going to let me use your car?"

"Of course. I'll pull it out of the garage for you."

"Thank you!" Amy kissed Grandpa Leo on the cheek.

Grams kissed Grandpa Leo on the other cheek. "You can have a second plate of the casserole for that."

"Then my devious plan worked." Grandpa Leo chuckled. "Where is my granddaughter off to?"

"First, I'm going to quit my job. Then I'm going to find that cowboy and make him mine."

CHAPTER TWENTY-ONE

Amy was impressed with how fast she packed her suitcase. Okay, maybe she jammed everything in there, but it didn't matter. Wrinkled clothes wouldn't stop her from conquering the world. She carried the suitcase down the stairs of the main house and out toward the driveway where Grandpa Leo had already uncovered his prized possession and pulled it out of the garage.

He handed her the keys and smiled. "Your chariot awaits you."

That made her smile.

Luke had said the same thing when he'd picked her up in his truck to come to Julian.

Amy stuck the suitcase in the trunk and closed it. "I've always loved this car and appreciated how much you've taken care of it all these years."

"When you take care of things, they tend to take care of you." Grandpa Leo rubbed the hood of the car with his hand. "Please take care of my girl."

Amy smiled. "I will."

"I was talking to the car." Grandpa Leo winked.

Amy stuck her arm out the window and waved goodbye as she drove away. A few minutes later she cruised through downtown Julian, enjoying the attention from the people on the street, the heads turning, the fingers pointing. She felt like a celebrity. Sure, they were looking at Grandpa Leo's car, not her, but she would let her ego enjoy the moment, anyway.

She passed Main Street Grub & Pub where she and Luke had their date. The thought of him got her blood pumping and made her want to put the pedal to the metal back to San Diego, but she had promised herself she wouldn't speed in Grandpa Leo's car.

Instead of going home first, Amy drove straight to the hotel to give notice. Surprisingly, quitting her job was easier than she thought. In fact, her boss told her the two-weeks notice wasn't necessary since he was thinking of reorganizing a few positions in the catering department, anyway. The timing was perfect. That was great news since Amy was ready to get Pie in the Sky moving in the right direction. Her boss wished her well and even said they would plan a special goodbye lunch to honor her many years of dedicated service and hard work for the hotel.

So far, so good.

Next up was finding Luke and convincing him they belonged together. That might be a tougher nut to crack, considering how her dad treated him, but she wouldn't give up. She didn't want to call him, though. Some things had to be done in person.

The problem was, to do it in person, Amy needed to find Luke. Not an easy task when she didn't have his address. It looked like she would have to pay another visit to Ed, the mechanical bull operator at the Double Deuce. He was friends with Luke and she was certain he would know where he was.

Later that evening, Amy pulled Grandpa Leo's Plymouth Belvedere into the Double Deuce parking lot and turned off the engine. She went inside, glanced around the place, then made her way toward the bull riding pit.

"Returning to the scene of the crime!" Ed said, laughing. "You lookin' for Luke again?"

Amy hesitated. "What makes you think that?" She pointed to the bull. "Maybe I want to take Buckshot for a spin."

"Hop on."

"I'm kidding. I'm looking for Luke."

Ed chuckled. "He doesn't work here—I've told you this before."

Amy placed her hands on her hips. "You know that I know he doesn't work here, but you're his friend. Friends have insider information, so can you please tell me where he is?"

"I sure can."

She waited a few seconds. "And are you *going* to tell me?"

"Sure am."

"This year?"

Ed glanced over Amy's shoulder. "He's right behind you."

Amy froze. "You mean like right *right* behind me?"

Ed shook his head. "Like right right *right* behind you. If he was any closer, he could give you a scalp massage."

Amy didn't know Ed well, but she had a feeling he was telling the truth.

Her heart rate picked up as she turned around.

Yup. That's him. The man of my dreams.

"Hi." She could barely get the word out.

Luke tipped his hat. "Howdy."

They stared at each other.

He fidgeted with his belt buckle.

She bit her lower lip.

Luke finally opened his mouth, surprise and doubt in his eyes. "How did you know I'd be here?"

"I didn't."

He hesitated and then pointed to Buckshot. "This is a good place to let off some steam."

"And you need to let off some steam?"

"I do." Luke touched the left side of his chest. "Broken heart."

"Maybe I can unbreak it."

He frowned. "It's broken pretty bad."

Luke's expression tore Amy apart. She didn't think their current situation was unfixable. This was all a big misunderstanding that needed to be cleared up.

"There's still a chance," Amy said.

"For what?"

"For us."

Luke didn't respond.

Not being able to read him made Amy more than a little uneasy.

Had she messed it up that badly?

"I didn't leave that money in the guesthouse to get rid of you," Amy said. "I was afraid you were going to tell me you wouldn't take the money because you and I . . . well, we had something between us. I left the money because we had a deal and you deserved to be paid, regardless of the outcome. I wanted to get it out of the way so we could move on."

"And I thought you wanted to move on in separate directions, since you only said *thank you* in the note." Luke held up a couple of fingers. "Two words. Nothing else. It seemed cold to me."

"I wrote that note and stuck it in the envelope with the money the night before we went to Julian. I didn't even know you then, and as far as I was concerned, it was a business deal."

"Your dad said you didn't want to see me anymore."

"He lied. He's got issues, and we're working on him. And I'm sorry I believed him instead of giving you the benefit of the doubt. I don't want you to think I'm excusing his behavior, either."

Luke nodded. "You moved all your stuff out of the guesthouse when I got back from the festival. What did you expect me to think about that?"

Oh. That.

That was a little more complicated to answer, but Amy needed to tell the truth. "Yes—I did move my stuff out, and that part wasn't my dad's fault. That was me. I was scared. I was mad at myself, actually. I was embarrassed for losing in front of all the people who know me. I was also worried what my dad would say. He needed me to win for the company and I disappointed him and everybody else. I needed to be alone, but only for a while. I'm not perfect and my hormones can be a little crazy at times, but the last thing I wanted was for you to leave. I promise."

Luke pulled his Stetson off, ran his fingers through his hair, and then stuck the hat back on his head. He was quiet, looking as if he were considering everything she had said.

Amy grabbed him by the hand and led him to a nearby stool, motioning for him to sit down.

Luke sat but still didn't speak, his eyes never leaving Amy's.

She slid onto the stool across from him. "I saw the interview." She smiled. "It said so much about you as a person. What you did for me and my family was *amazing*. Beyond kind. Saying thank you doesn't seem like it's enough."

"It is."

"I want to be with you."

There.

Amy threw it out there and held her breath, waiting for Luke's response.

She had to know if he shared the same feelings.

"I want to be with you, too," Luke said.

Nothing could have sounded sweeter.

Amy smiled and moved toward him.

"But . . ." Luke said.

She stopped in her tracks, confused. "But what?"

Amy waited for one heart-wrenching moment.

The way he said *but* didn't sound positive.

"Well . . ." Luke cleared his throat. "I think you should know I got a job and I'm moving out of San Diego." He shrugged. "Gotta go where the work is, you know? I don't think it should be an issue."

Amy stared at him.

Was he insane?

How could it not be an issue?

He was moving away.

It was an issue!

Luke said he wanted to be with her, so why was he leaving? Why were they even having this conversation? Did he think they would have a long-distance relationship? She'd tried that once and there was no way she would ever do it again. Long-distance relationships never worked.

Amy felt her heart breaking slowly.

She was too late.

Luke had already moved on and accepted a job far from her.

Her legs were shaking even though she was sitting.

But she wouldn't cry.

She didn't want him to feel guilty or pity her.

Her eyes betrayed her, burning, tearing up.

Please don't cry in front of him.

She looked away so he couldn't see her face.

"Whoa, whoa, whoa." Luke jumped up from the stool and caressed the side of Amy's cheek. "What's going on?" He pushed her chin up with his finger, concern in his eyes. "Are you okay? Why are you crying?"

She wiped a tear from her face and sniffled. "You're moving away. Do you think I'm supposed to be happy about that?"

"But—"

"I was pouring my heart out to you."

"Amy . . ."

"And then you say *hasta la vista*."

"Amy . . ."

"I know it was my fault. I shouldn't have—"

"Listen to me. Please."

"Why? I was trying to convince you that we had something special, but you had already made up your mind about the future. I feel like such a fool."

"Amy!"

A few heads turned in their direction.

She sniffled, then stared at Luke. "You don't have to yell. I'm right here."

"Sorry, but I'm trying to tell you something very important."

She crossed her arms. "What?"

"The job is in Julian."

Amy blinked. "I don't understand."

Luke smiled and wiped another tear from her face with his thumb. "I said my new job is in Julian. Ever heard of the place? Cute little town. Lots of apples."

She attempted to articulate something. Anything. "But, but . . . I thought you—"

"You thought wrong."

"I was scared. I didn't want to lose you."

"No chance of that."

"Julian . . ."

Luke grinned. "Yup."

Amy placed her hands on her hips. "I can't believe you did that!"

Luke threw his hands up. "What did I do?"

"You almost gave me a heart attack—that's what. Say you're sorry."

"I'm sorry," he said, chuckling. He grabbed her hips, pulled her close, and wrapped his arms around her. "This is where you belong. Right here."

Amy melted into his embrace. "You're forgiven."

"I know I said on television that I admired you, and I do, but it's much more than that." He wiped another tear from her face. "I love you."

She sniffled through her smile and squeezed him harder. "I love you, too."

"That's music to my ears." Luke leaned down, cupped her face with his big hands, then kissed her. Truly, madly, sweetly.

"Oh," Amy said, pulling away. "I also have news. I'm moving away, too."

He grinned. "To Julian."

Amy shook her head. "I should've known you would know."

"I told you before—General Maximus knows all."

"Oh, yeah? Does the gladiator know I'm the new CEO of Pie in the Sky?"

"*That* I did not know. Congratulations." He grinned. "All of this is happening, because we were meant to be together. I'm going to make you the happiest girlfriend in the world. And best of all, we're going to date like normal people. No more faking, no more betting, and no more competitions."

"There's nothing I'd love more than that." She reached up and kissed him.

"No more betting or competitions?" Ed snorted and interrupted their kiss. "What kind of nonsense is that?"

Hopefully, he hadn't been listening to their entire conversation.

"Sounds kind of boring, if you ask me." Ed gestured back to the bull. "A life without Buckshot is no life at all. That's my motto. What do you say? How about another ride for you two?"

They both turned and eyed Buckshot, then glanced at each other.

Amy shook her head. "It's tempting, but I'll pass."

"Good call," Luke said. "I'll pass, too."

"Really," Ed said, looking at both of them like they were freaks. "That's it? What if last time was a fluke and Amy should've won?"

Amy nodded. "You did *barely* beat me, but as long as you're not cocky, I'm okay with that."

Luke laughed. "Barely beat you? Ha! I recall kicking your butt."

"You will eat those words, cowboy."

"How will I do that if we're not competing anymore?"

She glanced at Buckshot again, and then back to Luke. "Double or nothing?"

"You're on!"

Ed clapped his hands. "Now you're talkin' my language!"

Luke gestured to Buckshot. "Ladies, first."

"No, no," Amy said, shaking her head. "After you. I insist."

"As you wish." Luke winked at her and then mounted Buckshot. After settling into position, he grabbed ahold of the rope with one hand, pointed his boots slightly out, squeezed his legs around the bull, and lifted his off-hand in the air. "Ready."

After another impressive ride, Luke finally flew off and landed on his back in the foam pit. He popped back up to his feet, brushed off his hands, and winked at Amy. "Good luck."

Amy patted him on the chest. "Thanks, but I won't need it." A few seconds later, she was up on the bull and lifting her off-hand in the air. "Let's do this."

The bull started to move slowly, dipping forward and then backward, like it always did.

Amy had as much confidence as she did the first time she'd ridden against Luke, but this time she was sure she was going to win.

After the ride of her life and being thrown from Buckshot, she smiled and got back up.

She turned to Ed, waiting to be declared the winner.

"Luke wins again!" Ed called out.

Amy crossed her arms. "No way! This thing is rigged."

"Come and look, if you don't believe me."

Amy walked over to Ed's electronic monitor and glanced down at Luke's time. Then she saw her own time.

She shook her head in disbelief. "He beat me by two seconds? That's ridiculous."

"A win is a win," Luke said, a smug but super-cute look on his face. He wiped his mouth dramatically. "I'm ready for that kiss, thank you very much."

"Fine," Amy said, stomping her feet toward him. "So you know, this is getting old. Are you going to win every time we compete? That's not going to make me happy."

"If it makes you feel any better, you've won my heart." Luke winked at her.

She sighed. "How can I be mad at you when you say things like that?"

"Sounds like you can't."

"Get your lips over here."

"As you wish." Luke took a few steps in her direction and held her in his arms. "I guess this is the part where you tell me about the rules. Okay, let me have them."

Amy shook her head. "Not this time."

Luke arched an eyebrow. "Seriously?"

"What can I say? I met this amazing man and now I'm a changed woman. Are we going to kiss or what?"

Luke grinned and then leaned down and pressed his lips to hers.

His kisses were sweet, like apple pie.

No. Sweeter.

He kissed her again.

And again.

Amy couldn't help but think of all the energy she had wasted trying to fight this. Trying to fight what was meant to be. Because there was something in her heart she always knew.

There was something about a cowboy.

But now, more than ever, she knew there was something about *this* cowboy.

EPILOGUE

One Year Later.

The woman stood in front of the microphone on the stage and waved to the audience below. "Welcome to the Julian Country Fair! It's so wonderful to have you all here again for our annual pie competition. And this year we have a sponsor, the Main Street Grub & Pub!"

Amy applauded, along with the rest of the audience. She was proud of Luke and what he had accomplished in one year.

"Coincidentally, last year's champion in the pie contest is one of the owners of Main Street Grub & Pub," the woman continued. "And he's here to say a few words before we get to the results of the competition. Let's hear it for Luke Jenkins!"

More applause and cheers from the audience.

Amy stood and whistled for him and then sat back down.

Luke walked across the stage and tipped his hat to the crowd. "Thank you. The Main Street Grub & Pub is proud to sponsor this amazing contest and we look forward to hearing who the winner is in a few minutes. We're also excited to let you know that the grand opening is coming up next week for our brand-new wedding venue and we'll be having an open house this Saturday. Stop by for free hot dogs and drinks and the ribbon cutting ceremony with the mayor. Okay, that's it from me. Let's get on with the contest. Oh, hold on! One more thing. So we're clear, I had *nothing* to do with the judging. I wanted to make sure you knew, because I'm sure my wife will win first place. I love you, baby!"

The crowd cheered as Luke blew a kiss to Amy and then left the stage.

And her heart melted on the spot.

She blew a kiss right back to him.

A lot had happened since the pie contest last year. Amy and Luke had gotten married. Pie in the Sky was thriving and the *Double, Double, Double* was their top-selling pie. And their first pumpkin patch was set to open the day after the grand opening for the wedding venue.

Grams and Grandpa Leo were going strong and still as cute as ever.

Jennie was still with Marcus and they had just announced their engagement.

Aunt Barbara met an oil importer and moved in with him. Oh—he lives in Morocco.

Even Greg was feeling great, traveling on his fourth cruise in twelve months.

As for Amy, she had the most amazing husband. She loved seeing Luke on stage. He had such a commanding presence. He could have been an actor, after all.

Luke scooted by people in their row, carefully trying not to spill his beer as he got back to his seat. "Excuse me, pardon me, excuse me." He sat back down next to Amy and kissed her.

She smiled and glanced down at his beer.

Luke held the cup in her direction. "Do you want a sip?"

Amy nodded. "Sure." She took two giant swigs, handing the beer back to him.

"Okay . . ." He looked inside the cup and then turned to her. "I asked you if you wanted one, remember?"

Amy nudged him with her arm. "And I told you I didn't."

He shook his head and chuckled. "Of course not."

She leaned closer and whispered, "And you shouldn't have told everyone I would win."

"I believe it. What else am I going to say?"

"I don't know." She pointed to the cup. "I'm getting nervous."

He laughed and handed her his beer.

"This is always my favorite part of the fair, the pie competition!" the woman said, gesturing to the pie tables. "And once again this year, we will be on *Good Morning America.* Wave to the cameras!"

The crowd cheered and applauded again.

"Showtime," Amy said, pressing her palm down on the top of her leg to settle it when she realized it was bouncing up and down.

Luke leaned closer and kissed Amy on the lips. "Good luck, baby."

"Thank you," she said, grabbing his beer and taking one more chug.

"Okay, then . . . let's get to the winners!" A judge walked over and handed her a slip of paper. "Honorable mention goes to . . ." She paused for the drumroll. "Marlene Jacoby for her cherry apple crumb! This is the second year in a row Marlene has won honorable mention with this pie. Please stand and take a bow, Marlene."

Marlene stood and waved to the crowd with a big smile as they cheered and applauded.

"And second place goes to . . ." She paused for another drumroll. "Christine Vangard for her salted caramel apple pie!"

Christine stood and waved to the crowd as they cheered and applauded.

Amy leaned toward Luke. "I'm either going to win first place *or* not even a place in the top three. Kill me if it's the latter." She pointed to the beer cup. "Anything left in that thing?"

Luke shook his head. "Sorry. My wife drank it all. And quit worrying." He kissed her on the cheek. "What did I tell you about General Maximus?"

"You know all."

"Exactly."

Her right leg bounced up and down again, so she pressed down on it to stop it. Then she crossed her legs and uncrossed them a few seconds later.

Hurry.

"And first place goes to . . ." The woman paused for the last drumroll.

Amy was sure her heart stopped beating.

"Amy Jenkins from Pie in the Sky for her new creation, the *Triple, Triple, Triple.* Come on up to the stage, Amy!"

Amy sat up straight, covering her nose and mouth with her hands.

I did it. I won.

Luke pumped his fist in the air. "Yes. I knew it!" He pulled Amy close, kissing her. "Congratulations. I love you."

"Thank you. I love you, too."

Amy waved to the audience and the cameras before heading up to the stage, walking tall, and taking in deep, satisfying breaths.

Her heart was full, and she was sure her eyes were going to be full, too.

She'd worked her butt off to perfect the recipe.

The hard work had paid off.

The woman pinned the winner's ribbon on Amy's shirt, handed her the first prize check, and posed for a few pictures with her.

Amy blew a kiss to Luke, thinking this was the happiest she had ever been in her life, after her wedding day.

"This is the first time in the history of the pie competition we've had a husband and wife win back-to-back years!"

Amy wasn't going to tell her that last year they weren't married yet.

"Please tell us what inspired you to make this pie and what exactly is the *Triple, Triple, Triple*."

Amy moved closer to the microphone. "Well, first thank you for this. It means the world to me." She paused for her heart rate to go back down. She took another deep breath. "This pie was inspired by my husband, Luke, who you all just met. Actually, he inspires me in just about everything I do, especially when he won this contest last year with his pie, the *Double, Double, Double*, which is available exclusively through Pie in the Sky. The *Triple, Triple, Triple* consists of three types of apples, three layers, and three secret spices. I dedicate this win to Luke, the love of my life. Thank you for making me the happiest woman in the world."

Luke smiled and waved at Amy, making her heart swell.

She waved back and walked down the stairs of the stage where he was waiting for her.

Luke wrapped his arms around Amy and kissed her. "I'm proud of you."

"Excuse me, Mrs. Jenkins." A man with a *Press* lanyard around his neck approached Amy. "If you could please follow me to the media tent. They'd like to record your interview segment."

"Of course." Amy kissed Luke on the lips. "Duty calls."

He grinned. "I know the routine. Be sure to say something nice about your husband on national television. I've got it. Tell them I'm the apple of your eye."

"Did you really just say that?"

"Yeah. I did. How do you like *them* apples?"

"My husband is quoting *Goodwill Hunting*. You're getting corny now. It's a good thing I love you, you know that?"

"Believe me, I know." He grinned. "It's a very good thing."

THE END

<<<<>>>>

ACKNOWLEDGMENTS

Dear Reader,

I hope you enjoyed *There's Something About a Cowboy*. I had fun writing this story and even enjoyed a trip to Julian, California (yes, it's a real place!) to walk around, research, and eat some amazing apple pie.

I would just like to take a moment to thank you for your support. Without you, I would not be able to write romantic comedies for a living. I love your emails and communication on Facebook. You motivate me to write faster! Don't be shy. Send an email to me at rich@richamooi.com to say hello. I personally respond to all emails and would love to hear from you.

Please LIKE my Facebook page and follow me here: https://www.facebook.com/author.richamooi/

Consider leaving a review of the book on Amazon and Goodreads! I appreciate it very much and it will help new readers find my stories.

It takes more than a few people to publish a book so I

want to send out a big THANK YOU to everyone who helped make *There's Something About a Cowboy* possible.

First, thank you to my amazing wife, the love of my life, Silvi Martin. She's the first person to read my stories and always gives me amazing feedback. I couldn't publish a book without her. Thank you, my angel! I love, love, love, love you!

Thanks to Mary Yakovets for editing.

To Paula Bothwell and Sherry Stevenson for proofreading. You rock!

Thanks to Sue Traynor for another amazing cover!

Thanks to Kimberly Kincaid, Claire McEwen, Deb Julienne, The Le Bou Crew, Author's Corner for help with the brainstorming.

To Rhonda Guthier and Kayla Guthier for helping me with farm research.

A huge thank you to my beta readers Robert, Maché, Marsha, Deb, and Krasimir for helping make this story even better.

Thanks to Karen Hunt Racket for coming up with the name Baa Baa Ganoush for the goat!

With gratitude,
Rich

FREE romantic comedy!
All of my newsletter subscribers
get a free copy of my fun story,
Happy to be Stuck with You, plus
updates on new releases and sales.
http://www.richamooi.com/newsletter.

**You can also browse my entire list of
romantic comedies on Amazon here:**
Author.to/AmazonRichAmooi

ABOUT THE AUTHOR

Rich Amooi is a former Silicon Valley radio personality and wedding DJ who now writes romantic comedies full-time in San Diego, California. He is happily married to a kiss monster imported from Spain. Rich believes in public displays of affection, silliness, infinite possibilities, donuts, gratitude, laughter, and happily ever after.

Connect with Rich!
www.richamooi.com
rich@richamooi.com
https://www.facebook.com/author.richamooi
https://twitter.com/richamooi

Made in the USA
Coppell, TX
04 December 2019